P9-DMV-826

A TRAP FOR FOOLS

AMANDA CROSS

BALLANTINE BOOKS • NEW YORK

IF

If you can keep your head when all about you
   Are losing theirs and blaming it on you,
If you can trust yourself when all men doubt you,
   But make allowance for their doubting too;
If you can wait and not be tired by waiting,
   Or being lied about, don't deal in lies,
Or being hated, don't give way to hating,
   And yet don't look too good, nor talk too wise:

If you can dream—and not make dreams your master;
   If you can think—and not make thoughts your aim;
If you can meet with Triumph and Disaster
   And treat those two impostors just the same;
If you can bear to hear the truth you've spoken
   Twisted by knaves to make a trap for fools,
Or watch the things you gave your life to broken,
   And stoop and build 'em up with worn-out tools:

If you can make one heap of all your winnings
   And risk it on one turn of pitch-and-toss
And lose, and start again at your beginnings
   And never breathe a word about your loss;
If you can force your heart and nerve and sinew
   To serve your turn long after they are gone,
And so hold on when there is nothing in you
   Except the Will which says to them: "Hold on!"

If you can talk with crowds and keep your virtue,
   Or walk with Kings—nor lose the common touch,
If neither foes nor loving friends can hurt you,
   If all men count with you, but none too much;
If you can fill the unforgiving minute
   With sixty seconds' worth of distance run,
Yours is the Earth and everything that's in it,
   And—which is more—you'll be a Man, my son!

—RUDYARD KIPLING

One

If you can keep your head when all about you
  Are losing theirs and blaming it on you

THE body was found early on Sunday morning by a member of the university security force patrolling the campus. He thought the man was a student or a bum sleeping it off on the edge of the path, but closer inspection rapidly disabused him of so comfortable an assumption. Looking up, he was able to spot the window from which the man had jumped or fallen. This was the Sunday after Thanksgiving, and the security force was at minimal strength. The officer called the central office on his walkie-talkie, and was told to stay where he was. Cursing, the second-in-command in security hurried over, trying to decide whether, if the report turned out to be accurate, to inform the police first or an officer of the university. Better have a look at the body, and then decide.

Butler, the second in command, annoyed at his boss's absence for the Thanksgiving holiday, met the officer outside the building known as Levy Hall. One glance was sufficient to assure anyone that here was death, but Butler bent over the body to make sure. No need to feel for a pulse. An unbroken fall from seven stories had left no doubt. The day was cold; what little blood there was had congealed. It occurred to Butler that there was remarkably little blood, considering that the body had landed on cement.

Butler decided to call one of the vice presidents of the university first—perhaps the one in charge of internal affairs. He also decided not to disturb the body with a search for identification; that was not bloody well going to be his decision. He had, however, no doubt that he recognized the man— a professor who had been around a long time and was well known to the security force for his petulance and pomposity. Using his set of master keys, Butler entered the building from which the man had jumped, fallen, or been pushed, God forbid, and used a telephone in the hall to call the vice president. "You'd better call the police," this gentleman answered, once his irritability at being aroused was assuaged by the seriousness of the message. "But wait ten minutes, which will give me time to get there before them."

You'd have time to get here before them, Butler thought to himself, if I'd called them half an hour ago. He had dealt with the police before and had few illusions. Still, this was death; they would probably have to send out someone from the D.A.'s office. He glanced at his watch, walked around to comfort the still-waiting security officer, and began counting off the full ten minutes. Butler followed orders: anything else was madness in this place of rich kids and overpaid professors. If he, Butler, got paid as much for as little work, he wouldn't bloody likely have thrown himself out of the goddamn window. But, of course, they were all wimps and, face it, the guy might have been pushed. (Kate Fansler, when she heard Butler's rendition of his reactions some time later, wondered about his saying "bloody." It turned out he had come from Ireland two decades ago, and refused to say "fucking" like all the other men. His reasons for eschewing the word were partly ethnic and partly devout.)

The vice president, looking disheveled and distraught, arrived in eight minutes by Butler's excellent watch—all this would go into the report—and was shown the body, which unfortunately (depending how you looked at it) he immediately recognized. It was Professor Canfield Adams, about whom the vice president, whose name was Matthew Noble, knew enough to tell Butler that he was the last man in the world likely to leap or fall out of a window; he was also someone who at least forty people connected to the university, and

3

God alone knew how many outside it, would have dearly loved to push. Butler went to call the police, and Matthew Noble went to the lavatory. Then the three of them, Butler, Noble, and the guard, huddled inside the lobby, awaiting the police, for it was a cold day and the building was unheated during the holiday break. Matthew Noble, trying to control his errant stomach by some rational thought, made a mental list of possible suspects based on motive alone. The exercise was strangely consoling.

The forty or so suspects on Matthew Noble's list were members of Adams's department, Middle East Culture and Literature, anomalously housed in a building named Levy after its long-dead benefactor; at the time of the benefaction the building had housed the various Romance languages and literatures, which had since distributed themselves about the campus, Middle East Culture and Literature having received a handsome donation to allow it to acquire and fix up its own building. That no tenured professor in the department taught Hebrew or anything to do with Israel had seemed awkward, to say the least, at the time of the move, but an old professor emeritus who had known Levy remembered that he was not a Zionist, which nicely settled that question. Adams was a professor of history occupying a name chair. In addition to the members of his department, there were not a few outside it who loathed him, to say nothing of some of those in the administration. At least, Matthew Noble thought, finding some meager food for consolation at last, we shan't have to deal with student and liberal faculty outcries about the death of a beloved member of our community. Adams was about as beloved as poison ivy and resembled that affliction in that one's resistance to it decreased with each attack. Damn.

Eventually, the police arrived; so did the president and a great many other people. Within several days it was determined that Adams had died, hit the ground so to speak, somewhere between eight and eleven o'clock on that Saturday night. Within several weeks, almost all the forty people on Matthew Noble's list turned out to have alibis more or less private, but strong nonetheless, depending, as one might expect for a Thanksgiving weekend, on the testimony of relatives and longtime friends, a handful relying only on the testimony of a husband or a wife or, as they now said everywhere, a significant other. A few hardy souls, fed up with Thanksgiving festivities, had been alone, but the plain fact of the matter was that no alibi was foolproof, and most were more than adequate.

The question of what Adams was doing in his office in the deserted university on that night was answered coherently by his wife, as soon as coherence could reasonably be expected of her. Adams had probably been worried about some work he was doing, the papers were in his office, he

5

had gone there. She was away; she could speak only of his usual habits, which often included weekend visits to his office. If he planned to meet someone, he had not mentioned it to her when they spoke to each other on the telephone.

The police were readily, if reluctantly, convinced that Adams would never have jumped. But might he have fallen? He was in his sixties; might he not have leaned out of the window and grown faint? Such a comforting solution could not be ruled out, but its unlikeliness increased the more carefully it was examined. There was a broad sill outside the window; there was no reason for him to have opened the window that wide on so cold a night if he had merely wanted air, or felt dizzy. How, then, had he been enticed to the open window to be pushed? The answer to that was equally simple: although he had smashed his head on landing, obliterating any previous wounds he might have received, he had probably been hit over the head in his office, or had a plastic bag thrust into his face, and was then shoved out. Did this not indicate a strong man as the murderer? Not necessarily; a vigorous woman would have had little trouble; Adams was a slight man, and women these days developed their muscles in health clubs, and perhaps in even more disreputable ways.

Because Professor Adams had recently served on a committee with Professor Kate Fansler, and because the most superficial investigation quickly revealed that he and Kate had long loathed each other with an intensity veering between cordial and bitter depending on how recently they had met, Kate was, with other professors similarly situated, asked to provide an alibi. She was, as it happened, the initial hope of the police as a secret suspect. The fact that she had some small reputation as a detective made her delightfully suspect on those grounds alone; the additional fact that she was married to a man who used to work in the D.A.'s office caused the police a momentary pause. But all of this turned out to mean nothing, for in those very hours when Professor Adams was hurling himself or being hurled over the sill of his seventh-floor window, Kate, along with a few thousand other people, was attending an Arlo Guthrie concert in Carnegie Hall. She was accompanied by her nephew Leo Fansler, a lawyer; her niece Leighton Fansler, an actress; and a friend of Leo who worked for a large banking firm. Kate Fansler herself was using, at the invitation of her niece, the ticket of another friend, also a lawyer, who had been called away suddenly to put in billable hours on a case. They had, moreover, met several acquaintances in the lobby and, erasing any possible doubt of Kate's not having been there the whole time, had been part of an altercation arising from the fact that Leo's friend had smuggled into Carnegie Hall a bottle of bourbon that the ushers had confiscated, not without enough general disturbance to draw to all the Fanslers and friend the attention of everyone in the surrounding

7

seats. The argument centered around proper behavior at a rock or folk concert, and resolved itself
into the only question concerning the manage-
ment: proper behavior at Carnegie Hall. To the
enormous disappointment of not a few, therefore,
Kate Fansler had an unbreakable, public, widely
witnessed alibi. That she was, as far as her char-
acter went, the last person likely to push anyone
out of a window carried little or no weight with
the police, or, if the truth be told, with the university administration. But presence at a public
concert, even a concert by a long-haired radical
like Arlo Guthrie who sang songs such as "This
Land Is My Land," "Amazing Grace," and "Alice's Restaurant"—he sang all three that night—
was an alibi. So that was that.

Thanksgiving had transformed itself to Christmas,
and Christmas to New Year's, and New Year's well
into the spring semester, with no solution to the
Adams murder in sight, when Matthew Noble
asked to see Kate Fansler in the provost's office.
Kate, who, as her niece Leighton frequently remarked, was not as great a detective in the ordinary course of things as she liked to make out,
went to the provost's office without a suspicion of
what was wanted of her. Adams's murder had re-
ceded, as university events seemed to do, before
the avalanche of midterms, student applications,
possible appointments to the faculty, and dissertation defenses. Kate walked into her fate as ig-

norantly, she afterward supposed, as Adams had entered his office on that fatal night. She was later to wonder if she would not, on the whole, have preferred grappling with an assailant on a windowsill. In that case, she was often to surmise, she might have had a better chance of winning.

For the first time in her university experience, she was not asked to wait for a meeting with an administrator but was immediately ushered into his office by a clearly nervous secretary. Administrative secretaries, who Kate often suspected of running the university while their bosses attended meetings and tasted power, tended to be cool without hauteur and pleasant without intimacy; that the provost's secretary was rattled boded no good. Could they be about to fire her? For what? Well, Kate thought, I shall set up as a private eye. That this was her thought upon entering the room was later seen by her nearest and dearest as evidence (and about time) of prescience. At which Kate snorted.

But at the moment, she took a seat—all the administrators except the one woman had risen as she entered, and all shook hands with Kate. The woman dean was a friend of Kate, and alone in this strange assembly seemed, though Kate hardly knew how she discerned it, amused by the proceedings. The others were whatever the absolute opposite of amused is. Matthew Noble, having issued the invitation, spoke first. "No doubt," he said, "you can guess why we have asked you to meet with us here."

"I haven't a clue," Kate said, her evident astonishment erasing any possibility that she was assuming an unbecoming innocence.

"Ah," the provost said. He was an extremely large man with an affable air that fooled no one and an ability to know exactly what was going on and to judge it fairly that fooled almost everyone. He was clever enough to listen to gossip and to believe a good part of it; he was brave enough to be disliked, and sensible enough to try to keep the number who disliked him to a minimum. All those on the faculty with more intelligence than ego hoped he would not leave his position before they did. Kate liked him, and sank simultaneously into her chair and bewilderment.

"You recall, of course, the unfortunate death of Professor Adams. More unfortunate, let us say within the sanctity of this room, in its manner than in the fact of it. Certainly, except by his immediate family, one hopes, and a few members of the faculty, he is unmourned; that has become painfully clear, and there seems little to be gained by denying it. At the same time, a university can hardly allow one of its most prominent faculty members, or in fact any faculty member, to be murdered without attempting to bring the culprit, as they used to say when I was a boy, to bay. I need hardly add that the police have got precisely nowhere. No; 'precisely' is an exaggeration—they have provided much negative evidence. They have, however, got nowhere in solving Adams's murder. We have decided, not easily"—and here he smiled at Kate and something close to a wink seemed for a moment to reveal itself—"to ask for your help."

This speech was followed by a profound silence.

Kate had time to see it coming. The provost, kind and clever man that he was, had given her time during his rambling speech to understand his meaning and consider it. While appreciating his courtesy, she had no intention of being persuaded by it. But he spoke again before she could.

"Matthew here," he said, gesturing toward Noble, "summoned you on behalf of us all; he was the first member of the university apart from members of the security force to see the body, and he has been bearing the brunt of the inquiries; I'm afraid *brunt* is the right word. Quite a few people have pointed out to him that you are known, only in the best circles, of course, for having solved a few crimes. We ask you, in the name of the university, to try to solve this one. We promise you all and every help we can give. It is clear that the police cannot possibly get anywhere. The prosecutor from the D.A.'s office is highly intelligent; in fact, he attended our law school. But the crime was a clever one and will require the investigation of someone who knows the university from the inside, so to speak, and who can move among its members without arousing suspicion. Or," he added, again with the flicker of a wink, "more suspicion than is her normal lot."

Kate sighed. Whatever her answer, a dignified request for the facts was the best way to begin and had the pleasing appearance of providing a sensible reason for her answer. She requested the facts. The provost turned to Matthew Noble, who cleared his throat and began stroking one of his eyebrows with a regularity that Kate found maddening and hated herself for finding maddening. She tried to listen to his facts while keeping her head down, as though lost in contemplation.

"You have heard about the universal alibis," he said. "The student newspaper reported them in tedious detail. Except for your own, none of them is absolute. That is, if we had a suspect, it might be proved that he—or she—had had the chance to slip away and back unnoticed. Only you were in your seat for three solid hours, intermissions included. We understand that you do not like intermissions, and always remain in your seat." Kate nodded, looking up and then resuming the contemplation of her hands in her lap. She held them still. She was not going to elaborate to this boob on her dislike of intermissions, nor explain to him that getting into the ladies' room during an intermission of any performance in any hall or theater in New York City was only possible, let alone bearable, if one's need was overwhelming.

"It is widely said," he continued, "that the

police aren't interested in motive. In this case that seems to be all they *have* to be interested in; there wasn't much other sort of evidence. But the police are hardly in a position to understand the motives or judge them rightly. Adams had fought with some members of his department to the point where they were barely speaking to him; there are a few who hated him with a virulence I used to find positively terrifying. But as we all know, in a university community that is far from meaning murder. Or was. I used to hear people say that the way to commit the perfect crime is to hit a total stranger over the head and disappear into the crowd. We are beginning to fear that where there are so many suspects you have the conditions of a stranger in a crowd. The case, in short, is unsolved. We turn to you.''

''I could list my reasons for refusing to do what you want,'' Kate said. ''They are many. But to give many reasons is to suggest a certain ambivalence or guilt. So let me merely say no.''

''We can't let you say that,'' the provost said. ''You are our only hope of solving this thing.''

''Then let it go unsolved. I understand about communities, and the finding of the guilty individual to return innocence to the rest of the community. But we have moved beyond those halcyon, or Agatha Christie, days. We are all guilty; Mr. Noble has already admitted as much. He has also admitted that the university community is well rid of Adams. So why not just announce that the best,

13

unceasing efforts of the police, etcetera, etcetera, have availed us nothing? We can all get on with trying to make the university a better place without him, a more enticing task.''

The dean of the professional schools, whose name was Edna Hoskins and whose demeanor comprised the velvet glove of maternal tolerance hiding the iron fist of determination, spoke next. ''I told them you would never accept so horrendous a job on the excuses they were offering. But my colleagues feel that to give away information is to give away power; I believe in an institution where shared information leads to shared power and responsibility. We will probably never agree on that, but they will have to agree with me this one time. Or so I assume.'' She looked around the room, her eyes meeting only resigned nods.

''There are two reasons that might persuade you to help us. One is that the police have a suspect, and they are going to do their best to pin it on him, as I believe one says. You will recognize that that would be a disaster as soon as I tell you his name: Humphrey Edgerton. He has no alibi, was heard to threaten Adams, and, alone in the entire university apart from the security force, possessed a key to Levy Hall, which he shared with some students.''

''Why on earth?'' Kate asked, appalled. Edgerton was black, outspoken about racial discrimination in the university, and had been known to come publicly close to blows with Adams, restraining himself only after Adams, older and in no shape whatever, had collapsed on the ground close to apoplexy and with a bleeding nose before Edgerton had touched him.

"Why did he have a key? Alas, because he needed a place to meet with black students and some faculty members on a regular basis. He insisted that it would be unreasonable to force him to go every Sunday, which is when they met, to get a key from the security office. Permission for this exception was granted, no doubt, if we are to continue this discussion in a mood of utmost frankness, which I certainly intend to do, because it would otherwise have seemed as though the administration was unwilling to trust a black faculty member with a key."

"Why hasn't he an alibi, if everyone else does?"

"He was trying to think something out, as he told his wife, and had gone for a long walk, heading downtown. I'm afraid, being black, he couldn't get a taxi to take him back uptown, so he took a bus and was gone even longer than he might have been. No one saw him, he met no one, he has no alibi."

"What's the second reason?" Kate asked, she hoped in a light tone. Edgerton taught literature, both American and Afro-American, as they were unfortunately still, like literature and feminist literature, separately dubbed. He and Kate were friends, at first more comrades because both felt marginalized by the university, lately friends be-

cause they had served together on many committees and had come to like and trust each other.

"There is no way to put this but bluntly," Edna
said. "Adams's wife, egged on by contingency
lawyers, is going to sue the university for everything from negligence to unexplained death—I
forget the technical terms. It seems if we can find
the murderer, she can only sue us for negligence,
if she can establish any. I mean, it isn't as though
the university had left all its buildings wide open
after many incidents of crime. The place could
hardly be shut up tighter, more's the pity; that's
what looks so bad for Humphrey, and doesn't look
that great for the university either.

"Let me say one thing," Edna interjected before Kate could speak. "I'm not going to pretend
to you, though some of these gentlemen"—the
word was very slightly emphasized—"wanted to,
that it has been easy to turn to you in the capacity
of chief investigator. But you must see, if you pon-
der the question as I urge you to do before giving
us any answer at all, that you have all the require-
ments: familiarity with the situation, and tact—I
know, I know, you're not famous for it, but you
know and I know that those who are famous for tact
are always known as tactful and never believed—a
proven ability at solving things, and the only absolutely unbreakable alibi among those who held Adams in less than perfect esteem."

Kate said, "You do realize that he might have
been murdered by someone we don't know hated

him, or even knew him well. He could have been murdered by someone in this room.''

''Touché. But we have to play the odds. And even if his murderer is wholly unknown to anyone, we'd rather trust you to establish that than the police, who, in my opinion, are likely to hit on the wrong person for the wrong reasons. A Zionist, for example.''

''You're not suggesting that Adams might have been working for the PLO?''

''I'm not suggesting anything. Adams was a specialist in Islamic history, and as far as I know had no passions one way or the other about Israel. But he certainly was against the study of modern Jewish history in his department, claiming that Israel only became a factor in the Middle East in the middle of this century. I didn't mean to raise this question particularly; I'm trying to suggest that we are sitting on a powder keg, to coin a phrase. We turn to you, as a woman of remarkable lucidity of intellect, to coin another.''

''I may do no better than Mr. Micawber. And, unlike Mr. Micawber, I may have a price.''

This was the provost's cue. ''We are prepared to pay it. For results, of course. Even for a damn good try—one that, say, eliminated the current suspect.''

Kate looked around the office. They all looked at her, waiting for a reply.

''Damn,'' Kate said.

Two

*If you can trust yourself when all men doubt you,
But make allowance for their doubting too*

EDNA HOSKINS swept Kate up and into her, Edna's, office, where she pushed Kate gently into a chair and rummaged in a cupboard for scotch. When they each had a glass, Edna raised hers: "To you, my dear. If you have tears, prepare to shed them now. I don't think Mrs. Micawber said that, but she might have. They planned for me to waft you off, by the way, so don't be alarmed about the ruffled male feathers we have left behind on the rest of the administration. At nearly six, we're all ready for a drink, but I for one prefer it in more congenial circumstances."

"You are the only congenial aspect of this circumstance," Kate said. "Edna, what am I to do?"

"What they ask. You haven't really got a choice, as I'm sure you've realized. Let me back up. You have a choice: you can do it, you can refuse, you can name a price for doing it.''

''I've never been paid for detecting.''

''You've also never been hired, within the meaning of the term. Why not ask to be paid in, say, student aid?''

''Suppose I don't find the murderer. Suppose, which is even worse, I find the murderer and don't want to tell them who it is. To say nothing of where I'm to find the time for all this in the middle of a terrible semester. Besides, I realized something in there that frightened me: I don't like the administration, and what is worse, I don't trust them. Which is probably why they don't trust me.''

''Rather sweeping, don't you think?'' Edna said, putting her feet on her desk, as was her wont, and sipping her drink. Kate regarded her with that affection women who have been through a good deal in the professional world feel for one another.

Kate said, ''I've liked the occasional administrator, even a male here and there. But frankly I wouldn't trust most of them not to choose expediency over principle every inch of the way. The definition of an administrator, at least of the old variety, is someone who knows what he can get away with. Every now and then they think they can get away with more than they can get away with: that's when you have student sit-ins, campus disruption, and changes in the administration. The occasional woman does what she can, if she's a gutsy woman, but she's got to play the game. Right or wrong?''

"Right *and* wrong. You're too old and smart for absolutes. I think you're afraid of failing. Afraid they'll all say, We knew she couldn't solve it; she's been overrated, like most academic women, particularly those of the feminist variety.''

"Oh, God," Kate said. "Can I get access to what the police have found?''

"Of course not. They intend to prosecute, and they're not about to give away their evidence, not until they have to. What games you can get your husband, as an ex-D.A., to play, I neither know nor want to.''

"Do you think the guys in there were counting on my asking Reed to help?''

"There are no straws to which they will not clutch. Including you as a detective. Why not talk the whole thing over with Reed?''

"Do you mind if I talk it over with you first?''

Edna sighed, refilled her glass and Kate's, and returned to put up her feet. She had raised four children with the help of a cooperative and loyal husband, and the security of that, and of having it all behind her, showed in her smile and in her assurance. She had been effective as a dean, and felt, in her late fifties, properly used. Kate trusted her. "My view, for what it's worth, is that you tell them you'll poke around. Try to see how the land lies. Demand introductions, which is to say command performances, from anyone you want to see over whom they, any of them, have the slightest influence. In other words, not only will they provide you with leverage; the minute they say lay off, you lay off. I would also," Edna answered with a mischievous look, "wave threats of publicity wildly around. It always serves to frighten away foxes and save the chickens. Don't ask me why."

"You refuse to advise me to refuse, flatly and finally."

"You've already refused to advise yourself; you'd have refused in there, if you were really adamant. I'm willing to use your own strength for purposes I support. And mine. But think it over. When you're ready, there is a certain amount of evidence the police have coughed up at the university's insistence. You can have all that. There's another reward you might consider. I promise you any member of the administration from the president down will talk to you instantly whenever you ask. Bound to be a certain gratification there."

"You," Kate said fondly, "can go to blazes. But before you do, find me the most communicative member of Adams's department. When I've talked to him, I'll let you know what I've decided to do."

"Would right now be too soon?" Edna asked. "I'm trying to impress you with our eagerness to be helpful in all possible ways."

"You've got a member of Adams's department hidden under your desk?"

"No, you idiot. I mean you don't need to talk to a member of his department; you can just listen to me. I may be dean of the professional schools, but Arabs and other rich folk wander in and out of my office, and I've had plenty to do, one way and another, with Adams's department. It differed from most departments only in that the members did not bother to preserve even the most superficial cordiality. They all hated one another, and only agreed when it came to keeping others out of their department. Of course they could never agree on hiring anyone. Adams was once chair for a couple of years. He insisted on it, claiming seniority and every other possible entitlement. They had to give it to him, but it didn't last even into the second year. He finally blamed his resignation on some personal problem at home with his wife, and thankfully disappeared, at least for a while. He demanded a semester's paid leave as the price of stepping down, which gives you some idea of how Adams worked. There's more, if you want it, but I honestly don't think you'll be very enlightened by talking to a member of the department. Still, if you ever want to, be my guest. Shall I find someone for you tomorrow?"

"Let's wait for several tomorrows, if not forever," Kate said, and went home to think.

Walking home, which Kate found always helped to clear her brain, she tried to remember, in some logical or at least chronological order, what she could of Canfield Adams. He seemed to her one of those circumstances of academic life, as mosquito bites were part of life in the summer, that had always been there and were part of the scenery, part of the activity, inevitable, ultimately uncontrollable. When you had said that he was pompous, long-winded, tiresome, a mass of personal mannerisms and twitches that horrified and fascinated his listeners, so that one could hardly bear either to watch or not to watch the jerking motions, the inevitable gestures, how far forward had you got? Most characteristically, he never seemed to finish a sentence, interrupting himself, winding himself into a cocoon of words, of digressions and digressions from digressions, until one wanted to end the sentence for him, or scream, or shoot him, or, Kate thought, shove him out of a window—anything to shut him up, or at least neaten up his syntax. Oddly enough, but like many tiresome academic speakers, he wrote well and clearly, if a bit given, pen in hand, to what he thought of as irony but what everyone else saw as sarcasm, petty perhaps but forthright.

They had both been at the university so long that she could hardly remember their first meeting; it had certainly taken place sometime in the middle or late seventies, when universities began to feel compelled to put women on every committee. Since there were many committees and few women, Kate passed through various stages of confabulation and consideration in a very short time. Adams had appeared early on—of that she was sure. He was the sort of man the administration in those days liked and trusted, which meant that he was narrow-minded, with all of the usual prejudices as to sex, race, class, sexual preference, and national origin, but also that he could be counted on to carry out the administration's desires. As the administration grew younger and a bit more forward-looking, he was less respected but not less in demand. The point of committees, after all, from the administration's point of view, was to prevent anything rash or awkward from happening. Certainly he could be counted on to stall indefinitely against changes in the canon, the rules, the faculty, or the calendar.

None of this would do, Kate told herself. Suppose, she thought, you had to describe him to someone—a jury, or a lawyer, or a judge. Will you please give us an account of the first meeting you can remember having with Professor Adams? It would hardly do to say that every time she found him in a room she blocked him out, not seeing, not hearing him for fear that her intense antagonism would show. Well, Your Honor, he lied, he was manipulative, he told you one thing and someone else another. But it was worse than that; he really could not believe that anyone who disagreed with him could be right.

Let's start over, Kate told herself. Describe him.

He was Germanic-looking, very fair, with that odd color hair that develops when very light blond hair turns white. At first glance, you might have thought him an albino; he seemed to have no lashes, and he had a beard the color of his skin. But he did not wear glasses, did not have weak albino eyes. Indeed, Kate found herself saying idiotically, one of my best friends is an albino. Adams thought of himself as a dandy and dressed accordingly; bad dressing was bearable; elegant dressing in evil men was oppressive. Some of my best friends dress elegantly.

She remembered a story she had heard. An excellent woman student, some years ago, told by him to go home and stay with her children, perhaps find a temporary job at the five-and-ten. Today such a remark would be funny, annoying at worst. Then it had been crushing. There was also a subtle form of sexual harassment; nothing he had ever been caught at. Simply that he had mainly female students, and that they had to behave to him in a certain way—flirtatious, grateful, pleasing, endearing, humble. Could all the women students have conspired to push him out the window in a united action first suggested by Agatha Christie? But that had been on a train. In this case there had been no evidence left in the room. Or had there? Really, she knew so little, it was preposterous to ask her to play detective.

No question about it, it was easier to seek wholeheartedly the murderer of someone you have liked, someone whose loss is evident, a general diminution of the humane. Why bother to find the murderer, if any, of a man whose demise one could only, if not rejoice in, at least accept with marvelous equanimity? For the same reason one did not believe in assassination or other kinds of violence.

Why pick on me? Kate thought. Why not hire a private eye or use the clout of the university to put some power into the police investigation? Am I being set up? But Edna would hardly go along with that. Her head remarkably uncleared, Kate reached home.

Where Reed was waiting for her. "I've heard," he said. "Edna Hoskins called me. I didn't promise her anything, but I said I was glad to know, and would try to talk it out with you. If you want to. Perhaps silence is what is called for at the moment, with generous lashings of gin and vermouth."

"Scotch," Kate said. "But it doesn't seem to be having any effect. I know what the problem is, though. It came to me, in the elevator here, after the doorman said you'd just come in. I think their asking me is a trick. I don't feel like a detective, let alone a detective the university would dream of hiring. I think their motives are despicable, and their hopes that I will fail and make a fool of myself into the bargain."

"Prophets in their own countries," Reed said, handing her a glass. "When is the only time you're

26

ever nervous before lecturing? A public lecture, I mean.''

''At my own university, of course. Doing things where they know you and are waiting to leer. Is that all it is?''

''A large part, I should think. Edna felt unable to convince you that the administration's need for you to undertake this, and their trust in you, while not unanimous, was strong and sincere. She didn't know how to tell you, so she told me. She said you have a built-in inability to believe compliments, and a dislike of being needed. She went so far as to say you married me because I didn't need propping up. Her making so personal a remark should carry a good deal of weight; it did with me.''

''You think I should do it.''

''I didn't say that. I need to know more about the case, what they know, what's expected. I just said that Edna said that your first reactions were probably not to be trusted. She may be right.''

''I don't know much more than you do, reading the papers and hearing me gossip,'' Kate said. ''The more I do know is persuasive and troubling.'' She told him about Humphrey Edgerton and the key to Levy Hall. ''To say nothing,'' she added, ''of the fact that Adams hated practically everyone; he once told me to my face that homosexuals belong in a sewer. Male, that is. I don't think he believed any more than Queen Victoria that women did that sort of thing. Adams thought

27

any woman would take a man, any man, if she could get him. There you are, you see. I start to say something and go on and on, with one nefarious report after another, but where is that likely to get me? I could of course begin by interviewing his wife; if she's mourning him, I'll think she's mad, and if she isn't, I'll think she's guilty. I'll just say no, shall I?''

"There is Humphrey Edgerton. Why not talk to him? Why not call him now? Perhaps he'd come over, or we could meet him, and that would help to settle your mind. Meet him alone, if you prefer.''

"I'll call him,'' Kate said. "Anything concrete to do, apart from rambling memories of the late and horrible Canfield Adams.''

"Good,'' Reed said. "The truth is, I'm more worried about you at this moment than I can ever remember being.''

"That makes two of us,'' Kate said on her way to the telephone.

Humphrey Edgerton was on the point of leaving to meet his wife; he would stop in for a short time. Glad to. He had something to tell Kate. And why, Kate thought, do I instinctively know that it is bad news? Because it's that sort of bloody situation, she thought, unconsciously echoing Butler of the security force.

Humphrey accepted a chair and a drink. "You'd better sit down,'' he said to Kate, who was pacing

the room. "The fact is, I didn't have the key to
Levy Hall. I'd given it to a student who wanted to
hold a meeting there of the black student caucus.
Of course, the administration will say that I should
not have helped the students to get a key; the police will say that she gave it to someone or used
it herself to murder Adams; and I can't even swear
to the total absence of what my mother used to
call hanky-panky because Arabella is what I call
an activist when I'm talking to the world and a ded-
icated troublemaker when I'm talking to friends.
Arabella's like an army in today's world: essential
that you have it; even more essential that you don't
use it. She is also an ardent supporter of the PLO
and of divestment of companies who do business
in South Africa. I know that neither of these
seemed to concern Adams, except that he probably told her she knew nothing about the PLO and
that he did not believe in divestment. In short, I
can't give them Arabella, of whom I wish I felt
surer than I do."

"Well, that's wonderful," Kate said. "Hunky-
dory, as *my* mother used to say. Did you stop by
to cheer me up, cheer me on, or warn me off?
Just clear up your message, if you can."

Humphrey laughed. "Clear messages belong to
another age. I think this mess has to be straight-
ened out, and I think you're the best person by
several light-years to do it. I know and love you
too much to suggest that you will be thanked, or
even end up with a sense of accomplishment. In

29

this world, we do what we have to do, and we look for rewards, if any, in the work itself and the love of friends. That's absolutely as rhetorical as I intend to get. If you were a black man at a university you'd know exactly what I mean, always remembering that the work is tiresome and the friends frequently at odds.''

''That,'' Kate said, ''is the best double message I've heard in years. Almost the paradigmatic double message. Thanks a lot, as my young relatives say.''

''You've got to do it, Kate. You know it, I know it, Edna Hoskins knows it, and I suspect Reed does. I'll give you all the help and support I can. I don't say that lightly, but when I say it I mean it, and I'm saying it. Usually we haven't a choice. Some people like Adams have a choice and always make the wrong one. Sometimes we have the illusion of having a choice. None of the above applies here.''

''Where do you suggest I begin?''

''I'd begin with the guy's wife; soften her up for future questioning. Meanwhile, I'll round up Arabella and we'll come to see you soon. I think there's a certain amount to be got out of her, and we'll get it. I better go now or there's a certain amount my wife will get out of me; she doesn't like waiting in restaurants, and who's to blame her.'' He kissed Kate solemnly on both cheeks, shook Reed's hand, and rushed away.

30

"Well," Reed said. "I'm glad that's settled. What about dinner?"

"Reed," Kate said. "Let's go up right now and have a look at Levy Hall."

"On an empty stomach?"

"You're not in Napoleon's army," Kate said. "Yet," she added ominously.

Levy Hall was one of the older buildings on the campus, built in more gracious and expansive days. Its ceilings were high, its stairways broad and open to the large lobby: fire laws had been less stringent then also. Adams's office was on the top floor: Kate and Reed walked up, not trusting the elevators in a deserted building at night. They had first completed the usual routine for gaining admission to a locked building after hours: one had to have previously applied for what is called a key card (most departments applied en masse for their professors). When one picked up the building key—always attached to a large piece of wood—one surrendered one's ID card, to be reclaimed when the key was returned. Kate had done all this, and then more. Putting the administration's cooperation immediately and unreasonably (for she had not yet officially accepted the job) to the challenge, she had requested also the master key to all the doors inside Levy Hall. To her intense annoyance and disappointment, for she was looking, as she admitted to Reed, for any complaint, the man in charge of the security office,

31

after examining her ID and his own instructions, handed her the master key.

She and Reed had gone together to the building, proving, as Reed pointed out while opening the door, that no one necessarily expected the claimer of the key to enter alone the building to which the key belonged. "Please note also," Kate said, "that if someone I knew, particularly someone I knew had legitimate business in this building, came along as I was opening the door, I would certainly let him or her in. Or them. We can never know if Adams let anyone in that way."

The main floor with the lobby was designated the third floor, in a manner common to buildings erected on a hill. Rather than call the lower floors minus one and two, the entrance floor was dubbed whatever number it had in the usual sequence starting at the bottom. Kate and Reed climbed four floors to the seventh. Adams, however, as Kate pointed out to Reed when they had reached the seventh floor, had an office facing the opposite way from the entrance, meaning that he had fallen the full seven floors to the concrete path below.

Adams's office was attractive. He, or someone, had added an Oriental rug and drapes to the stark room; these, together with the crowded bookcases and the easy chair and lamp, gave the room a far homier air than was usual in university offices, at least those at this university. That suggested, Kate told Reed, that he worked in his office in preference to working at home, indicating a stronger

32

argument for his coming there at such an odd time. Kate, like many of her colleagues, used her office solely for business: seeing students, holding office hours, holding the occasional meeting.

They both walked over to the large window. An air conditioner was in the very top, but the lower pane opened readily, easily wide enough to accommodate a person contemplating, or being forced to contemplate, defenestration. The outer sill, eighteen inches wide, certainly precluded the possibility of anyone's carelessly falling unaided from the window after a dizzy spell. Kate supposed the window had been found open after Adams's death, but that was just one of the many facts wholly unknown to her.

Kate sat down at Adams's desk, inviting Reed to rest on the easy chair. "We've got to decide," she said.

"Wrong pronoun."

"Right pronoun. If you can't persuade someone to give me a few of the facts the police are clutching to their bosom, or suggest another way I might get them, I can't even begin. Have they tidied up this office? Did the desk seem to be rifled through? That sort of thing."

"I'm certain the university can persuade the police to tell you all that. All they'll withhold are statements by suspects. I didn't have a chance to tell you before," Reed added, "but I'll soon be off for a few weeks, to Holland and beyond, to that legal conference I told you was looming. It's now

33

here, unfortunately, and is international and important, so I can't beg off. I won't be here to help at first."

"Pooh," Kate said. "I'll probably not even have begun in a matter of weeks."

Reed said, "If you begin, you'd better begin right away. That's the only advice I can give you. Start off with a rush, and learn everything you can."

"Why do you think I should do it? And don't say it's my decision, in that holy way. I'm asking for advice, damn it."

"Because, as Humphrey wisely observed, you have a choice, and I think you've already made it. There are jobs one only refuses at one's peril. And don't ask me what peril; you know perfectly well what I mean."

"He sat here," Kate said. "Adams sat where I am sitting. You know, he has enacted, or had enacted upon him, a common academic fantasy: that certain faculty members would rid the world of themselves by some precipitous act, like flinging themselves from a window. The objects of these fantasies are often aging professors, intellectually stagnant, with no offers from anywhere else, only the determination to stay until the last possible moment before retirement. And of course with Congressman Pepper's new law, a man of Adams's age could stay on forever. Not that many actually do or are expected to, but the possibility looms. Suppose

someone, some otherwise quite agreeable someone, simply acted out that general fantasy?''

"The name of that is murder, and it is unacceptable in a decent society. As you very well know."

"Yes," Kate said. "I very well know. But I
cannot rid myself of anathematical thoughts about
the Adamses and their kind. Isn't that a nice word?
I was determined to use it, and I have. When are
you leaving for Holland?''

"In a week. Come on; let's have dinner. Or do
you think if we sent out for Chinese food, one of
those intrepid fellows on a bicycle would manage
to deliver it up here?''

Kate, having locked up the office and the building, returned the keys and reclaimed her ID. The
noticeable attention and courtesy of the man in the
security office suggested that the administration was
both hopeful and ready. As she and Reed walked
out onto the largely empty campus, Kate remarked
that she always felt lonely walking around the university in off hours. "Perhaps Adams felt lonely
too," she said. "Maybe that's why he fixed his office up to be more cozy and homelike.''

"That's perceptive of you, my dear. And unusual.
There's a sentence from John le Carré I admire: 'It
is the pardonable vanity of lonely people everywhere to assume that they have no counterparts.' ''

"I fear my vanities are unpardonable," Kate
gloomily remarked. "Certainly as regards failure
in this case.''

Three

If you can wait and not be tired by waiting,
Or being lied about, don't deal in lies

KATE began the next morning with Butler, the man in the security force who had been in charge the night the body was found. He, obviously acting under orders, related all he knew of that night more or less graciously, always allowing for the fact that his views on women and where they belonged were not inadequately reflected by the laws of the Irish Republic. He brought Kate carefully up to the arrival of the police.

And then what? Kate asked. Had Butler gone up with them to Adams's office?

Butler had. One of his standing orders was to remain with the police at all times when they were on campus, which mercifully had been fewer in recent years. The police had taken the elevator (being, Kate decided, unlike her and Reed when they had looked at the office, in radio contact with would-be rescuers). The office door was shut and locked; Butler had had to open it with his master key. The window was wide open, and the curtains had whipped out the window when he opened the door. Some papers were flying about. The police brought in special people to look for blood, fingerprints, or whatever they looked for; as far as he could tell they had found no blood and enough fingerprints to suggest that half the university had been through the place. They sealed the office, subsequently unsealing it when their investigations were over but asking that no one be allowed to enter (a request that Kate knew, and Butler knew she knew, had not been followed; the police might give their orders, but Butler worked for the university).

"You see, Professor [for she was a professor, much as he disapproved], there wasn't anything there that wasn't caused by the wind blowing about."

"No other signs of struggle," Kate added. "No sign of the desk or any other part of the room being searched?"

"No *sign*; which doesn't mean nothing was searched, just that I saw no sign of it. The police opened the desk drawers, and they certainly didn't see any sign of disorder, more than you expect in desk drawers, if you follow me."

"Could we sit down?" Kate asked. Butler, acquiescing with a reluctance sufficiently muted to

37

allow for its being adamantly denied, led her from the central security office, where they were talking, into a small room in the back. He shut the door. They both sat down, Butler behind his desk.

"Mr. Butler," Kate went on, "I'm asking you to help me; you don't have to like me, or even put up with me for long, but without your hearty help we're both going to be talking too long and to little purpose. I need to know all you noticed but are not required to say; all you think, but don't want to say; all, anything, to do with Professor Adams that might, whether you can see it or not, cast some light. I'm mentioning it frankly, because without your help I feel stymied before I start. To make me completely discouraged you've only to continue in your proper, polite, ungiving manner."

"Holy Mother of God," Butler said.

"Of whose help, or anyone's, I would be glad," Kate responded; "at the moment, especially of yours. And do stop calling me 'Professor.' If I call you Butler, you can call me Fansler or, if you prefer, Kate."

"As in *The Taming of the Shrew*," Butler said. "I read my Shakespeare, though I'm no bloody professor. My name is Patrick."

" 'Yes, by Saint Patrick, but there is, Horatio.' *Hamlet*."

"Is what?" Butler asked.

" 'Much offense,' " Kate said. "A man has been murdered."

"May have been. Or flung himself from the window, being the follower of an unholy religion."

"He taught Islam; I don't know that he followed it. They say professors of religion are the only ones who don't believe what they teach. Do you think he did—fling himself from the window?"

"If wishes could kill, he did."

"Widely disliked, was he?"

"I shan't call you Kate, I shall call you Professor. You call me Butler. But I'll help you if I can. Not because you persuaded me, which you didn't, but because I've remembered what a sorry man he was. That Professor Adams. I'd rather work with a woman, and that's the truth."

"Good," Kate said. "First of all, what does it mean that you are second in command; what does the position entail?"

"It means that I'm in charge when the man in charge of the whole shebang isn't here." His tone implied that this should be obvious even to a professor. "It also means that I tend to be here on weekends and holidays and other times when someone has to be in charge of the security force and the chief has first choice on when he takes off."

"I see," Kate said. "Now, could we go back to the beginning? When you got the radio call from the guard who found the body. And from there back to anything else to do with Adams over the years. Not all at once, but in what I'm afraid you will regard as too many conversations.''

Butler stared at her. ''The call came, as you very well know, early on the Sunday morning after Thanksgiving. Adams was lying on the pavement below his window. I recognized him at once; he'd been a proper pain in the belly and no mistake. But I haven't seen a shred of evidence to say he was pushed, and that's the truth.''

''Not in the office; not anywhere?''

''No. And the only thing the police have let us know, and bloody noble of them it was I must say, is that there was no evidence of foul play: he wasn't shot, knifed, poisoned, or bruised. If he was hit to knock him out, there was no evidence of it left. Could I ask you a personal question? Two?''

Kate nodded.

''Are you married?''

Kate looked at her ringless hand. ''Yes, I'm married. I don't wear a ring, or use his name, but for all that I'm married. A long time now. Are you?''

''She wears my ring, uses my name, and lives on what I earn.''

''You said two questions.''

''Why are you doing this job? If I'm picking up the right signals, you disliked Adams as much as I did; as much as everyone did. Why look for his murderer?''

''A good question. I'll make it even better. Why should I help a university that I have been forced
40

to honor less and less as the years go by? Not that that means I despise it. In the beginning I honored it this side of idolatry.'' Kate looked out of the window, from which she could see a large sweep of the campus. "I don't believe in murder; I don't condone it. I can't put it any more elegantly than that. And I believe that if we don't get as near as possible to the truth, someone will suffer for it, perhaps many people. I'm not sure the truth exists, but I'm looking for it. Sorry not to sound more convincing; I haven't even convinced myself.''

"I can't see murder's so much worse that what goes on around here,'' Butler said. "Homosexuality, fornication, drugs, disruption—all mortal sins. You can't pick up a black male casing the campus because you might infringe his civil rights, when it's rape and mayhem and burglary he's after. And the campus priest arguing against the cardinal. What's the murder of a no-good man to all that?''

"We are going to have to agree to disagree on many things,'' Kate said. "Perhaps we can argue; perhaps we can convince one another. As I said, I need your help and I'm asking for it. If you can't or won't, then tell me. I don't think I'll get very far without you. I don't think I'll try.''

"I'll bet you're a Democrat. I bet you didn't admire President Reagan.''

"Right on both scores. Despite all our differences, I think we both know what we mean by our word, and keeping it, and helping each other toward working out this thing. Can you make a bargain on that? Please think.''

''I always think. The answer is yes, not because you've persuaded me, but because if you give me the credit owing, it'll be a feather in my cap.''

''Good reason,'' Kate said. ''Now, can we begin over again, Butler?''

''Shoot, Professor.''

Kate settled back in her chair, stretched out her legs, and collected her thoughts. Butler went to the door, opened it, and shouted through it for a couple of coffees. ''Black, I suppose,'' he said. Kate nodded. ''To be expected. I take mine with sugar and cream if I can get it, milk if I can't. Now, where were we?''

Where they were, as Kate told Reed later that evening, was back at the beginning: with a body and no idea how it got there or why.

''I may have Butler's help because he disliked Adams even more than he dislikes me,'' Kate said. ''We're both infidels of the worst sort, but Adams was arrogant and dishonest into the bargain. And I have a feeling Butler may be important, not just for easing my way in and out of buildings, but also because he's around at night and on weekends, just when there aren't too many people about, and it's nice to know someone on your side is firmly in charge in the security office. Also—I know this will sound crazy and probably is, but despite all the disdain I have for the security force in general, there's some way in which I want someone not an academic or an administrator on my side.''

"If you say so," Reed said. "I only hope he's there when the real murderer decides to go after you."

Kate paid no attention to this. "There is one other hopeful sign," she said. "When I called Adams's wife—widow, I should say—and identified myself she was perfectly willing to see me. Apparently being a woman professor with a little reputation and strong connections to the university count more than I had realized. I'm going to see her tomorrow. When do you leave?''

And they went on to talk of other things.

Kate called on Cecelia Adams the next day at lunchtime, in between university commitments. Cecelia was not at all what Kate had expected, but then few were, as Kate had lived long enough to learn. Yet just as you begin to rejoice in the individuality of human beings, there appears some creature from central casting so predictable that all rejoicing ends. Like Adams, perhaps.

As it happened, Kate was struck almost simultaneously with the astonishing vision of Cecelia herself, all girlish ebullience and heavy makeup, and a representation of Cecelia confronting Kate as she was shown into the Adamses' living room. The portrait of her hostess was so large, lifeless, flattering, and god-awful that Kate had consciously to keep herself from shuddering before it. The woman in the picture seemed even to be almost simpering, but not quite, as though she was mocking herself. But that, surely, was unlikely.

"Myself in younger, happier days," Cecelia Adams said. "Can I fix you a little something?"

Kate declined demurely. A strong drinker, Kate rarely drank in the middle of the day and never with those who drank to stop themselves thinking. But she accepted some ginger ale and tried to meet the oddly convivial mood of her hostess.

"If you want to talk about Canny, I'll have to get another," Cecelia frankly said. Kate's face must have reflected momentary puzzlement, because she added, "My dead husband, you know, Canfield. We called him Canny, and believe me, he was. Cheers."

Kate smiled at her. Cecelia was clearly a narcissist of sorts, devoted to herself, her beauty, her desires for expensive objects and rich clothes, but she had a refreshing openness the more valued in a university community, where egoism was disguised as scholarly rigor and enjoyment as intellectual despair. Kate knew there were many couples in academia as close to the ideal of marriage, that is, the continuing possibility of conversation, as were to be found anywhere, but academia also offered many cases of marriages without any sort of interaction, let alone conver-

44

sation, and this looked like having been one of them. Still, one never knew, and Kate was not a leaper to conclusions when she worked at it. "How was he canny?" she finally asked, which seemed better than the question of why Adams's wife seemed nearer rejoicing than mourning.

"You know, liked to think he had it all figured out, that he had superior knowledge, not to say wisdom. But he wasn't half as canny as he thought; if he were, he'd never have married me."

Kate looked her question.

"Well, my dear, he thought that, unlike other men similarly inclined, he could marry a much younger woman who wasn't after anything but the glow from his beautiful soul. It's easy enough pretending you're after their aging bodies, but convincing them that you would love them as dearly if they were without what my dear mother called a pot to piss in is a wee bit harder. But not that hard. That's why I called him Canny."

Kate stared at the woman for perhaps a full minute while she pranced gaily about the living room, rearranging objects and flaunting her small, full body as though she were a voluptuous gazelle; Kate, who was tall, felt enormous and even clumsy beside this merry widow, who did look quite capable of bursting into song. Kate decided to stop being a green thought in a green shade and said, "Mrs. Adams, are you trying to impress me with your motive for murder or merely enticing me into

45

a thoroughly improper conversation? If the latter, I'm ready now.''

"Call me Cecelia; everybody does. I added the first syllable. Just Celia sound so *ordinaire*, if you know what I mean; over before you've even begun. I didn't really have a motive for murder; if he'd lived another year I'd have had the whole kit and caboodle, instead of only two-thirds. Anyway, I have a lovely alibi; I was away visiting a dear uncle of mine who had some sort of seizure. He's quite well-off and with no noticeable heirs, so I dote when called upon. It never hurts. I was in the clear sight of at least half a dozen people every minute of the day and night, not to mention being three thousand miles away in sunny California. You do look very professorish, I must say, though beautifully thin. Lots of breeding, clearly, not like me. I clawed my way to the top, or as near the top as I could get these days, and I'm ready enough to admit it." Saying this, Cecelia held out both hands to Kate, their backs outward so that the long nails and white nail polish were in clear view. White, Kate supposed, not to suggest clawing.

"Cecelia," Kate said, allowing a certain imperious note to come into her voice, as was clearly expected by her giddy hostess, "might I ask a few questions? I am, as you say, professorish, and, like all professors, have convinced myself that I have an orderly mind when it comes to essentials. Of which, at the moment, you are certainly one."

"But you talk wonderfully," Cecelia responded, perching in a chair like a restless child forced to be nice to her elders. "Ask away."

"I take it you married Professor Canfield Adams recently?"

"Not recently, you know. Just more recently than his first wife. Canny was in his late fifties. I'm a teeny bit past forty, no use lying to a professor who's also a detective, is there? His first wife was his age and got dumped shortly after Canny and I met. That is, he thought he dumped her. She clearly dumped him, but I never saw any point in arguing the question with Canny. She wanted only to provide for her children out of Canny's inheritance from a beautifully rich papa, but we fooled her, Canny and I. Her children will probably sue, but possession is nine-tenths of the law, isn't that what they say?"

"And they also say that legal fees are nine-tenths of what you possess, but it may not come to that. What did you inherit, exactly, if you don't mind telling me?"

"Longing to, as you very well know. First I got this apartment. Joint ownership, so it goes to the spouse, who is me. Then I got him to build us a little love nest on the Mediterranean, where he liked to go to feel part of the Middle East. That is also joint, therefore to spouse. Then I got him to set up a little trust fund, income to me, and to the 'children' on my death. Since the 'children' are not that much younger than I am, they'll have quite a wait; I certainly hope so. He also left them each a tidy little bundle, which I would have added to the trust, income to little me for life, if I'd had time enough. But someone bumped him off. Not something I'd be likely to do, at least not at that moment. So there you are.''

Kate had to make an effort not to gasp. *Refreshing* was certainly the word for her, which had no doubt occurred to Cecelia long before this. ''Are you sure someone 'bumped him off,' as you put it; that is, pushed him from an office window to his death? You don't think there's a chance he fell, or climbed out onto the sill in a moment of dementia?''

''Not a chance, Professor, you can take it from me. He was as protective of himself as a turtle with its head and feet pulled in. He was afraid of drafts, let alone standing outside a window in November. No. Someone tipped him out. Too bad, really, on the whole.''

''Did you spend Thanksgiving together?''

''But of course, Professor. Together with sons and the sons' wives and kiddies. Both of his sons hated me, and usually took Thanksgiving turnabout, but this time they all came, don't ask me why. Don't ask me why they ever came. Not because they loved him, and not because they were worried about their inheritance, I don't honestly think, just good old middle-class guilt: you're supposed to want to see your father once in a while. I think they really felt that once every two years was enough, and frankly so did I. I was hoping they'd go back to turnabout, and now we don't ever have to share another turkey; how's that for a jolly thought?''

"What about Christmas?''

"Hark the Herald Angels and all that? We spent Christmas in our little Mediterranean hut, warm sun and just us two, the Christmas roast and pudding being cooked and served by a native woman there who cleans for us and is paid next to nothing, like all the other local servants, at least compared to servants around here. The hut was supposed to induce romantic powers into old Canny, but I'll tell you frankly it hadn't worked lately. Still, we could cuddle. And no damn grandchildren. I don't care for children, do you?''

Kate, who didn't, decided to ignore this. "Cecelia,'' she said, "I do appreciate your frankness. If everyone I talk to is as frank as you, I shall have this whole business cleaned up in a week. Were you this frank with the police?''

"What do you take me for? Woman to woman is one thing; the damn police are another. I sat like a proper widow, wiping away a tear and talking about the shock of it all. It was a shock, of course, and that helped a good bit. I don't mind being frank with you, but if you quote me to anyone I'll deny the whole thing and call you a liar; I'm good at that.''

"What do you think most people thought of your husband?''

"They thought he was a shit, which he was. But you could get around him if you just flattered him enough. I once heard a quote from some Englishman in politics; he said, 'You always flatter everyone, and with royalty you lay it on with a trowel.' I laid it on with a trowel for my royalty. But he only got on really well with a few girl students, who slimed all over him, and a few young men who thought he could give them a shove on their way up the academic greasy pole. Don't mean to sound offensive, Professor, that just came out sounding odder than I intended. Not that I talked to many of those who hated him, of course, but he came home all the time with accounts of committee meetings when he thought he triumphed and showed someone or other up for a fool, and you didn't have to have a Ph.D. to know they probably hated his guts and thought him an ass besides. But I can't tell you anyone who was likelier to have shoved him out the window than anyone else. I'd help if I could; they shouldn't have picked this moment to do it, so I'm not as grateful as I might be."

"Did he socialize with many of his colleagues?"

"If you mean did we have them here to dinner, we did once in a while, usually when the department paid for it because they were looking someone over, as Canny always put it. We were asked out sometimes, and Canny realized we had to ask people back. But he hadn't any real buddies, if

that's what you want to know. There were those
who agreed with him, of course, but usually he
had something nasty to say about them; he had to
feel superior, you see. It was part of his canni-
ness.''

''You left the day after Thanksgiving for California; had you any idea what he intended to do,
or whom he planned to see, while you were
gone?''

''Well, I know he had some page proofs from
his new book, and he meant to get them done. He
was going to work day and night when I was gone.
I suppose he must have needed something to check
them with and that's why he went to the office.''

''I see,'' Kate said. It was the first she'd heard
of the book. ''Where are the proofs now?''

''That's what's so odd, you see; he mailed them
off to the publisher on that Saturday. Sent me a
card in sunny California to tell me so. Of course,
my uncle only sent it on after I'd come back, hearing the next morning about Canny's death. Do you
think the book had something to do with it?''

''It doesn't seem likely, not if he'd mailed the
proofs off before he went to his office, which he
must have done; do you know who the publisher
is?''

''Harvard. He was very proud of that. He'd belonged to one of those snotty clubs at Harvard,
and some woman at Harvard sued to get in. You'd
have thought she was after his balls, if you see
what I mean. Everything was Harvard to him. So

it had to have the best press and the one he wanted to do his book. He's quite an authority on Arabs, or their religion, or history or something; I never really listened, to tell you the truth. After all, it was all a long time ago, wasn't it? You ready for a little something yet?''

''Yes,'' Kate said, ''I am. More than a little something. But I mustn't have it, I must go back and teach. May I take a rain check and come some other time for my drink?''

''Any time, Professor,'' Cecelia said, sashaying to the door and flinging it open. ''I'd like to hear what you have to say for yourself when you let your hair down, if you ever do.''

Kate, passing through the doorway, waved a feeble farewell as she walked down the corridor to the elevator. She had trouble bringing her thoughts back to the French novels of the eighteenth century on that day's reading list. What in the world would Corinne have made of Cecelia? Or Heloise, if it came to that? What Rousseau would have made of Cecelia, Kate had no doubt whatever.

Four

Or being hated, don't give way to hating,
 And yet don't look too good, nor talk too wise

THE phone was ringing as Kate opened her office door. It was Dean Edna Hoskins. "How about a drink and conference today?" she asked.

"ESP," Kate said. "I was just about to call you with the same suggestion. Have you ever met the late Adams's wife?"

"No," Edna said. "Have I missed something?"

"That's putting it conservatively. That woman convinces me that life holds more possibilities than are dreamed of in my philosophy. Also my views on women are beginning to resemble Hamlet's. I shall need you as a counterforce." And Kate rushed off to class, to be followed by office hours and, if possible, an hour's necessary devotion to her mail.

She had worked herself around to this last task, and was just beginning to open her accumulation of mail when she came upon an invitation to a meeting of the women faculty at the university. The notice had been sent some time before; the meeting was the next day, and Kate had not even opened the letter, let alone replied to it. But she would go. And as she wrote this into her calendar an idea began to take root in her mind that she determined to try out on Edna. She also hoped that Edna would have a few powerfully helpful suggestions.

When Kate, at the end of what seemed an unnaturally long day, finally collapsed in Edna's office, Edna said, "I've been thinking about your task, and having a few ideas. I also rather thought you might like to talk with someone reliable, sympathetic, and aware of the prevailing conditions. Straight or with water?"

"The ideas or the scotch? I'll take them both straight."

"That kind of day, was it? Well, we have chosen a stimulating rather than a restful life, and I for one wouldn't have it any other way. Even the thought of going quietly home to write a book doesn't appeal anymore. I think I know too much now about everything to feel capable of writing about anything. Tell me about the Adams woman."

"She despised him and was methodically separating him and his children from all his money. She had her eye on a bit more, though, and I think while she might very well have contemplated murder, she would have timed it differently. Also she was three thousand miles away, cultivating a not-impoverished uncle. Her fingernails are white, her hair is blond, and I have no doubt that before too long her face will be lifted, her breasts filled with silicone, the fat removed from her thighs, and if she goes the whole hog, she'll have her bottom ribs removed to give her the illusion of a narrow waist."

"Did she tell you all that?"

"Of course not; I am just foretelling based on an account of an aging woman I heard not too long ago. If you can't pass for young no point in living, seems to be the message. I think it's the message Cecelia Adams has received loud and clear. It certainly worked with Canny; that's what she called her late husband because in her opinion he wasn't."

"Drink up," Edna said. "I can feel your confidence in humanity oozing out of your toes. Was she very unpleasant?"

"Not in the least. Thoroughly pleasant woman. Said if I quoted her to anyone she would flatly deny it; she probably will. That puts her one up on her late husband, who lied without knowing it or warning you. Edna, I feel like an archaeologist who set out to unearth some ancient center of civilization and came up with Sodom. Or do I mean Gomorrah?''

''What you mean is that you've uncovered more unpleasantness without getting noticeably further in your task.''

''That does put it more clearly. Would you mind reminding me again why I've undertaken this 'task'?''

''To keep the police from making dreadful mischief, to keep from stoking the fires of racism, which are already smoldering in this city and probably in this university, and to discover the truth or a reasonable facsimile thereof. And don't tell me you don't believe the truth is discoverable. Facts are discoverable; their interpretation varies. That's the whole point, isn't it?''

Kate said, ''The whole point is how I'm to find facts, let alone interpret them. I've been one day on the job, have found someone with the almost perfect motive and the perfect alibi. Perhaps she's lying about the virtues of waiting for the whole bundle. Maybe she just couldn't stand him anymore and hired someone to shove him out the window. Heaven knows, she knew enough about him to manipulate him into anything short of jumping himself. I see ahead of me endless conversations with endless people who loathed Canny, as I shall henceforth inevitably think of him, and would have pushed him if they'd had the chance. And how much further along shall I be? And why do I give a damn anyway? And don't talk to me about Humphrey Edgerton or his black pupils. If they didn't do it we shall get them a good defense lawyer.''

''Being accused of a crime is horrible even if you're not convicted of it. I'm not putting that well, but . . .''

''Of course I know what you mean,'' Kate said. ''Might we together, now, concoct a rational plan that I can undertake and, having undertaken, abandon when it fails, saying I tried?''

''My suggestion,'' Edna said, putting her feet up on the desk, ''is that we try to recruit people to help you. I don't just mean people you can question, like Butler and the delectable widow; I mean a team of helpers.''

''Rant on,'' Kate said. ''We ask the president or one of the vice presidents to appoint a committee. If that's your plan, why didn't you suggest it in the first place before you involved me?''

Edna said, ''There's a meeting tomorrow of the women faculty at the university. I don't suppose you noticed.''

''I did notice, just today, and planned to suggest to you, that is, to ask you about the possibility . . .''

''There you are then,'' Edna said.

''Suppose they say no?''

''We can't hope to get all of them; but a few, who will let you know privately, can ask questions or provide information in different departments;

---

they can spread out and give you what I believe is known as wider coverage.''

"What about the departments with no tenured women?''

"We're not just talking about tenured women,'' Edna said. "There are too many departments without tenured women. But there are almost none these days without untenured women. And the younger women, when they're not solely on the make, are often quite gutsy, or so I've found. What about you?''

"I have a definite sense that the administration will not be happy about this little maneuver,'' Kate said, beginning to see its possibilities.

Edna said, "They chose you; they have to let you do what needs to be done. Anyway, try it tomorrow and see how the meeting goes.''

"Which means telling them what I'm doing; it'll be all over the university.''

"It will be all over the university in any case. And as I said earlier, confidentiality—except in very special situations—was designed by the male power structure to defend its ranks. And if you quote me on that I'll take a leaf from the widow and deny I ever said it. Let's have another.''

Meetings of the women faculty at the university were, by the end of the eighties, an almost routine matter. After years of tense meetings to strengthen the presence of women faculty on the campus, the tone of women's conversation with one another at meetings such as this had changed, becoming both more theoretical and more personal, certainly gayer. Those women professors who found it useful to talk to women colleagues in other departments and schools, who did not mind being identified as women faculty (as opposed to faculty, pure and simple and, apparently, neuter), met on an irregular but continuous basis. Not all the women professors came all the time. But those who liked the fact of the meetings wrote notes to explain why they had to miss this meeting or that, and tried to attend at least one or two a year. Those who did not like the fact of the meetings, though regularly invited, never responded and never came, except for a woman professor who once wrote an impassioned note pointing out that if women "made trouble" they would never endear themselves to the administration. The response—that women had made no trouble for centuries without endearing themselves professionally in any notable way—had no apparent effect. The most senior women, with rare exceptions, neither came to the meetings nor approved of them. Kate's very favorite among these was a woman philosopher who, uniquely in that department's history, had received tenure because the then chairman, an immensely famous philosopher, was living with her and threatened to leave the university if she was not granted tenure. There were several wonderful ironies to this situation: the first was that the woman was indeed brilliant

59

and ought to have gotten tenure in her own right were that possible for a woman philosopher at that time; the second was that she totally disapproved of feminism in all its forms, and said often and emphatically that any woman with the proper talent could make it as she had. Not a single feminist in the university was ever able sufficiently to abandon her "gentlemanly" scruples long enough to face this aging philosophy professor with the essential anomaly of her situation.

The meetings were very informal; sherry was offered. Kate, who loathed sherry, always drank soda water and savored the conversation. After some general milling about, the woman who called the meetings and who was, uniquely in a university where everyone had too much on her plate to undertake organizing anything else, the spirit and mover behind the meetings, asked the group if they wished any subject for general discussion or if anyone had any matter she wished to bring up. Usually those with an agenda item in mind had called the day before to say so, as Kate had done after her meeting with Edna Hoskins. She now waited her turn, watching with great affection and admiration the woman who ran the meeting.

Miriam Rubin was in her early sixties and had allowed herself to age without changing her style in any way. She was a tiny woman—a number of people called her Dr. Ruth after an equally short doctor who gave sexual advice on television, and indeed it was not hard to picture Miriam doing the same thing. She was the most downright person Kate had ever known, with a wonderful indifference to what anybody thought of her, except the few she had decided to love. These included her husband, her children, a few old cronies (all male) from early days at the university, and the Jack Russell terriers she and her husband raised in their exurban home. Kate adored Miriam, who, lacking all discretion and political know-how, gave the gift of courage all unawares, and was equally unaware of how widely she was loved.

There was some discussion of previous matters that had, as Miriam said, come before the meeting; she then announced that she would give the floor to Kate, who had something of great moment to impart. Miriam was incapable, or at least unwilling, to use last names, her personal fight against the pomposity of male pedagogy.

Kate said, "You all know that Professor Canfield Adams died after a fall from his office window late at night. The police believe that he was pushed; in short, that he was murdered. The university administration is unhappy with what they believe to be the police's conclusions, and with the altogether disturbing situation of the cause of death never being satisfactorily established. They have asked me to investigate the matter as best I can, and to let them know if I can discover any explanation of Adams's death." Here Kate paused and took a large breath.

AMANDA CROSS

"That's as much of this speech as I have prepared," she said, putting down the paper from which she had been reading. "I want to say several more things, but haven't figured out the clearest way to say them. I want to ask you not to discuss this widely, since to do so can hardly benefit me or the chances, if any, of revealing the murderer. In almost total contradiction to this, I want to ask you to help me by learning and recalling anything that might help me in this difficult and unpleasant task. Anything you have heard about Adams, or about those who worked with him or had anything at all to do with him; any fact or gossip or anecdote, no matter how important or unimportant it may seem. There might have been incidents that strike you not only as regrettable, but as unimportant. I would still like to hear them. And I would like to hear any stories that you can evoke from your colleagues, students, the staff, and anyone else who may have known Adams or have had anything at all to do with him. Anything, however minor it may seem, may be helpful when put together with other bits of information. I assure you that I shall not reveal the source of any information I may use, and that I will not reveal anything if it serves no purpose in the solution of this murder."

By now there was a good deal of stirring among the group, and Kate held up her hands: "Only a moment more. Let me say that I would not ask for this help if I didn't need it, and that I am personally convinced, even while loathing this job,

62

that there is great danger in doing nothing and letting the police and the D.A. proceed in the way they seem to be going. Innocent people will suffer, and regrettable incidents will occur. I badly need help, and I ask for it from a group of people whose ability to help one another I have long experience of as well as admiration for. Those of you, particularly the younger women from departments other than mine, who may wish to speak to me about helping without having any particular piece of information to offer, please do get in touch with me. I'll try to answer your questions, but as you will soon see, my knowledge is almost nonexistent.''

"Did the administration ask you to do this?" someone called out.

"Yes," Kate said. "I was hardly responsive to the request, but I have become convinced that they do wish to solve this crime, and that their motives are not unduly ulterior or hidden. Dean Edna Hoskins has been in on the administration consultations and has urged me to undertake this task. I do so, as she understands, with great reluctance."

Miriam Rubin stood up. "Could you give us the facts that you *do* have?"

"Gladly," Kate said. "But you probably know them all. They are few in number. Professor Adams's body was found, by a member of the security force, lying on the walkway below Levy Hall early on the Sunday morning following Thanksgiving. Adams had fallen or been pushed

63

from the window of his office on the seventh floor. There was no sign of any injury other than those caused by hitting the cement after such a fall, but some previous cause of death might have been concealed by those injuries, or might be difficult to trace. No one was seen entering the building with Adams, or leaving it, or at all. He might have jumped or become dizzy, opened the window for air, and fallen, but the outside sill is too wide to make either of those accidents probable; Adams is widely considered unlikely to have committed suicide. His widow and I are the only two members of the university or his family with unbreakable alibis: she was in California, and I was at an Arlo Guthrie concert during all the possible hours in which the fall could have taken place. My alibi, together with the fact that I have worked unofficially on one or two cases, made me a likely candidate as chief investigator, the first counting more heavily than the second.''

''How did Adams get into Levy Hall?'' someone asked.

''Using his key card. He stopped at the security office to pick up the key and leave his ID. That is how it is known when he was last seen alive— except, as they say, by his murderer, or by someone else who has not come forward.''

Everyone sat in silence. Kate suggested that anyone wanting to talk to her call or write her either at home or in her office; she gave both addresses and numbers. She again promised confidentiality about anything she was told. Then she sat down wishing, not for the first time, that these meetings served something other than sherry or soda. She poured herself more soda water. Many of the women came up to her and promised to think about their relations with Adams or any stories they had heard. Others had never met him, but promised to ask around. One woman Kate did not know marched up to Kate and told her that the request was wholly immoral and unacceptable, and that she would have nothing to do with the investigation. Kate thanked her for her frankness. "Believe me, I wanted nothing to do with it either," she added. But the woman looked unbelieving. And who is to blame her, Kate thought. It is what we do that speaks for us, not what we say.

She said as much to Reed on the telephone to Holland later that night. "Well," he answered, "it's a place to begin. I would also try to find out what Adams did on that Saturday."

"He hardly knew it was the last day of his life. He probably stayed home working on his proofs, and went up to the office to look up a questionable footnote."

"Probably. But someone met him there, or at least knew he was going there. It seems unlikely that anyone met him accidentally, accompanied him to his office, and pushed him out the window on an impulse. It's possible, but unlikely. And it's

65

only possible if the person had a long-standing grudge, which ought to be discoverable.''

''There's always the homicidal maniac. Not fair to the reader of a detective story, but they do turn up in life, don't they?''

''Not in a murder like this, I don't think. No, whoever did this knew the victim and hated him. That's what's going to make it possible to solve the crime. And that's why the wider the net you throw, the more leads you will catch.''

Edna, when she telephoned to find out how the meeting had gone, said much the same thing. ''Did you mention what an all-around SOB he was?'' Edna asked.

''No, I didn't. I figured they either knew it or would soon find it out, and I didn't want to sound as though I were organizing a vendetta or something.''

''Wise woman. Something will come of it, you'll see.''

''Meanwhile, Reed thinks I should find out what Adams was doing all day Saturday. He wasn't in the library; it was closed.''

''Perhaps that's why he had to go to his office.''

''Edna, suppose I put an ad in the student paper asking to hear from anyone who saw or met Adams on Saturday?''

''The student paper is just what we don't want to encourage into writing about the case yet, or finding out you're investigating it. That may be unavoidable after today's meeting, but I don't think putting an ad in their paper is just the thing at the moment. Wait a minute though. Suppose I put in an ad for anyone on the campus that weekend, Thursday to Sunday, for a study of possible causes of depression during holiday seasons. I'll ask them to respond to the Psychology Department, where I have a friend who owes me one. That should give us a start. And I meant to tell you, I've thought of something else. I shall talk to my priceless secretary, and ask her to talk to the other priceless secretaries. They are all the sine qua non of the university, the 'without which not.' What they don't know is hardly worth knowing. I'll suggest that they might want to pass on any tidbits of note. And from me to you, my dear.''

"Edna, you should be running this investigation.''

"Of course, Kate. With your help. That's how, on a larger scale, I run the university. How *did* you think administration worked? I'll put the ad in tomorrow.''

Kate realized she was in for a spell of waiting, a condition she had never relished. But it occurred to her, as it had so often recently, that as the years go on a sense of deep patience comes over one; one seems to know the virtue of ripeness, and the danger of rushing events. She had recently heard the story of a demonstration by a biologist: he and his class watched a butterfly slowly emerge from its chrysalis, and with agonizing deliberation expand its tightly folded wings. The scientist, impatient, helpful, stretched the wing and damaged it forever, teaching his students the while. Inevitably one must learn to wait.

Meanwhile, Kate settled down with the one material contribution the administration had yet made to Kate's endeavors: a folder of all the records the university had on Professor Adams. Kate flipped through it in amazement. The yearly updates of his *curriculum vitae* were to be expected, as well as a record of his salary and sabbaticals. Included also were all newspaper and magazine clippings that mentioned Adams and the university (it was to be concluded that the university employed a clipping bureau), and a list of all the classes Adams had taught, with their registration figures. (Kate thought: I never knew they kept a record of that.) There were also copies of all his letters to any member of the administration, usually complaining about some suggested change of which he disapproved; requests for favors, from traveling money to appointments of his friends as adjuncts; student complaints about him (rather a large number, it seemed to Kate, but she didn't know they kept these either). There were various technical details, such as the bank into which his salary checks were automatically deposited, the insurance he carried, additional payments into his pension fund, and all the details of his family, his children, his marriages, his medical claims. Then he had been, for a two-year period, chair of his department, and there was a cluster of correspondence from that time, including his increasingly petulant letters to various deans and vice presidents about departmental matters as well as university policy, about which he felt newly required to complain in his capacity as head of his department.

Of course Kate wondered if they had a similar record on her, and recognized that they must, except that she had never been chair of her department, and had never, as far as she could remember, written a letter of complaint to anyone in the administration. Whether or not letters complaining about her had been received she might not ever find out unless murdered, but she was pleased to discover that she was not in this regard particularly interested, or even decently curious. She thought, I grow old.

So too had Adams grown old. The records of his life scarcely recorded his breathless sense of aging, but that sense was palpable: in his resentment of the young, offered privileges he had not had; in his growing pettiness; in his marriage to a woman almost twenty years younger than him and wholly nonintellectual; in the sparsity of his publications, the recording of small notes and necrologies in his *vita*, sure evidence of faltering powers and interest. Under the heading ''Works in Progress'' signs of what Kate took to be the new book began appearing several years before. To have published it would have been important to an unproductive scholar like Adams, whether or not it was well received. The latest copy of his *vita*, however, did not list this book as "forthcoming from Harvard University Press," as one might have expected. Given the time it took publishers to process a manuscript into a book these days, to say nothing of the time earlier spent having the manuscript read, readers' reports consulted, and discussion of the book held by the various boards who ran university presses, Adams must certainly have known by last year's *curriculum vitae* that his book was scheduled to be published. Perhaps he was keeping it under wraps, as a surprise for his doubting colleagues. Kate made a note to get a copy of the manuscript of the book as soon as possible; she realized that she did not even know its title, nor would she have known it was forthcoming but for the remarks of the divine Cecelia.

After leaving a message to herself to request a copy of the book from Vice President Noble, to whom all requests from her were officially to go, Kate called it a day. The question is, she thought, can I call it a beginning?

Five

If you can dream—and not make dreams your master;
  If you can think—and not make thoughts your aim

KATE, waiting for news of Adams's book, and for her and Edna's requests to the women's groups to filter through and find a willing subject, decided to get in touch with the sons of Canfield Adams. She was looking through her folders of material (courtesy Vice President Noble) to see if she had their addresses, when the phone rang. "Is this Professor Kate Fansler?" an aging male voice inquired. Kate admitted that it was. "You don't know me," the man went on to say. "I'm an alumnus of the university, what I believe is euphemistically known as a 'friend.' That means I give money in certain amounts. My daughter has a friend on the faculty, and tells me you want to speak to anyone who knew Professor Adams at all well. I took a good many courses with him, and would be glad to give you what information I can; I can't imagine it will be of any use, but my daughter urged me to call. My name is Witherspoon, by the way: Gabriel Witherspoon.''

Networking is a wondrous thing, Kate thought. "I would very much appreciate talking with you, Mr. Witherspoon. Can we set a time now?''

"Why don't you come here to tea?'' Mr. Witherspoon asked. "You'll save me a trip to the university, and I can offer some excellent pound cake made by my cook.''

"That would be lovely.'' They set an afternoon convenient to them both; Kate jotted down the address, Park Avenue in the seventies, and decided to check it out. There is absolutely no point in showing up at strange addresses after one phone call to find oneself hideously embarrassed at best, endangered at worst. She called Noble's secretary, who promised to get back to her promptly with the information. While she was at it, Kate also requested the addresses of the Adams sons. Whatever comes of this, she thought, I shall once in my life have the experience of snapping my fingers and having people hop to it, not good for the soul as a regular thing, but fun as a unique experience.

Indeed, the secretary was back on the telephone with commendable speed. First, the whereabouts of the Adams sons. Kate made a note of this, also hearing with satisfaction that the university would pay all travel costs incurred during the investigation. Then a word about Mr. Gabriel Witherspoon, which Vice President Noble would like to have with Professor Fansler personally. Oh, whoopy-do, Kate thought, either a big donor or an embarrassing nut. Before Noble was thirty seconds into his disquisition, Kate knew it was the former. "I don't know how you got to him," Noble said, pausing just long enough for an explanation, which Kate did not offer, "but he's one of our 'best' donors. I do hope . . ." His voice trailed off. Kate was soothing, but not acquiescent.

"I shan't try to frighten him away from the university as a haunt of murderers, obviously," she said. "But I've got to hear what he has to say, and ask him questions. If you or any others in the administration are having second thoughts about this investigation," she asked forcefully, "now is the time to say so. I shall bow out with pleasure. But if I am to continue, you've got to help me without constantly warning me off. Can we get that quite clear, or do you want time to think it over before I go any deeper into this? I can always beg off to Mr. Witherspoon and anyone and everyone else."

Noble was conciliatory, but clearly nervous. Kate decided to drive the point home. "If you think that you can solve this murder, or let us say this mystery, without stirring up memories, resentments, ill feeling, you're being naïve, and I urge you yet again to reconsider. I must talk to people, and what I discover, or what people start reconsidering and discussing, may not be all that you would wish talked about in the higher academic echelons. But this problem is not going to be cleaned up delicately and behind the scenes; few problems are. So do be certain; shall I wait for you to consult others?''

''No,'' Noble said with some asperity. ''That won't be necessary.''

Kate was aware that there had been a certain mockery in her voice, unsuccessfully suppressed. People always thought secrets could be held inviolate through thick and thin; Kate had learned that even through thin they were unlikely to remain hidden; through thick, as one might denote a murder investigation, there was no chance of keeping the lid even partly on.

Mr. Witherspoon had suggested the day after tomorrow for their tea, and Kate appeared at the door of his Park Avenue apartment house exactly on time. The doorman called up to announce her, and told her to get off on the seventh floor, thereby indicating that Mr. Witherspoon occupied a duplex in this very elegant building.

A maid in a white apron opened the seventh-floor door to Kate, who was immediately back in her childhood—except that as a child, visiting her friends, she would have gone to the bedroom floor and been admitted into the heart of the family life. Downstairs was for adult entertainments, sherry in the library, formal dinner in the dining room. Her friends in those days, more often than not, had dinner on trays in their bedrooms—cozy, infinitely intimate and privileged. There was often, Kate remembered, a younger brother who longed to join them but who could not lower his dignity by asking. The nicest of Kate's friends included him, demanding half of his dessert as price, not because they wanted it, but because it preserved his pride to let him buy his way into their company. One could never pretend really to *want* a younger brother's company, nor could one reveal pity: how the subtle politics of the nursery returned to one, Kate thought; she, only with brothers very much older, had marveled at the variety of family dynamics.

The maid showed Kate into the library, where Mr. Witherspoon rose to greet her. Kate wondered if he had been a small brother in the circumstances she remembered; did they, in short, share another world? If Mr. Witherspoon knew that they did—and this was very likely because the Fansler name was well known in the higher reaches of Waspdom—he did not let on. She had come to see him as a professor and scholar, and he offered sherry and information in the library. Kate's knowledge of the rules of the game forced her to accept the sherry.

"When did you study with Professor Adams?" she asked, pretending to sip from her glass and then putting it down.

"That," Mr. Witherspoon said, "is a long story. I retired at sixty-five and determined to pursue what had always been an interest of mine: the Crusades. Is that an interest of yours?" he asked, whether hopefully or not Kate could not quite determine. She shook her head emphatically but, she hoped, in an interested way.

"I went to the graduate history department at the university, determined to get an M.A. while learning more about the Crusades. The chairman of the department very kindly consulted with me at considerable length—(I bet he did, Kate thought; primed by the development office if not the president himself)—and said that, unfortunately they were not that year offering any courses on the Crusades, nor indeed anything for beginning graduate students but the most general courses about the Middle Ages. But, the chairman said, had I ever thought of studying the culture at which the Crusades were aimed: Islam? I hadn't, but he was very persuasive. He said that as a matter of fact there was a professor at the university who would exactly suit my interest, if I could just turn it around, so to speak. That, of course, was Professor Adams. The chairman did warn me, in the nicest possible way, that Professor Adams was not overwhelmingly popular with the undergraduate students, but he thought I might find him suited to my purposes. So, to make a long story short, I agreed, and took myself off to Professor Adams. I found him wonderfully informative on Islam, and

I studied with him for years, going on to earn a Ph.D., all but the dissertation. What they call an ABD these days, I understand.''

''How many courses did you take with Professor Adams altogether?'' Kate asked. She was enchanted with Gabriel Witherspoon. His making a long story short plunged her back yet again into her parents' world, even as his apartment had done.

''Quite a few. I can look up the records and tell you the exact titles, if that would help. He also provided what I guess you could call tutorials: private instruction, in his office. I found him a very interesting man, and, as a result, I quite abandoned the Crusades and have a now long-standing interest in Islam. I was disturbed to hear of his death.''

''Had you been in touch with him recently?''

''The university has several dinners a year for donors—though they always pretend they have some other purpose—and Adams was often asked to sit at the table with me at those times. I was certain the university requested, perhaps even demanded, his presence, but he did not strike me as the sort of man who would have come if he hadn't wanted to. One of the times he came to such a dinner he brought his new young wife, but she found the proceedings dull, and he never brought her again. I was a little surprised that he had married her, but these May-December alliances are commoner than one likes to admit.'' Thus, graciously, did Mr. Witherspoon indicate his disapproval of the marriage. "I take it," he added, "his wife is not in any way suspected in connection with the death." This was not really a question, more a hope, and Kate confirmed it.

"She was in California at the time. Could you give me some sense of Professor Adams, of the man, of what you thought of him not just as an Islamic scholar, though I would like to hear that too, but as an individual. You must have formed rather clear impressions over the years, and while you might not want to proclaim them in the ordinary way, my questions are not, alas, in the ordinary way."

"I see you don't like sherry. And it comes to me that I offered you tea, and ought not to try to palm off sherry on you. Will you excuse me just a minute, while I see if I can round up some tea for us?" As Kate smiled he walked from the room, marking, as Kate knew, a step into his confidence. She had, one way or another, passed muster. Her ability to do this with the likes of Witherspoon was one of her strongest suits as an investigator, unwilling as she was to admit the fact, or at least to dwell on it. Despite her often outspoken differences with the establishment, she was one of them by birth, and they sensed it.

Witherspoon returned to await the tea and continue the conversation. He removed Kate's sherry glass to a side table. "I understood why Adams wasn't a popular professor; I understood it partic-

78

ularly well because it was what made him appeal to me. He didn't want to be touched personally, he didn't want to admit any weaknesses, or reveal anything at all about himself. He was, as I am, or used to be, of what they called the 'old school': proud, appearing hard and unfeeling, but underneath it all, afraid, particularly of emotion or of letting anyone get too near you. The problem with Adams, I think, was that he was in the wrong profession for that particular kind of personality. In business or law one can be open about cases or problems without having to slip over into personalities; I rather think it is not so easy to be impersonal in the academic world. You will be able to interpret this better than I. What I mean is, you can still consult up to a point in law or business, the consultation is expected and does not indicate weakness. But in the academic world, or at least as Adams saw that world, one couldn't consult one's colleagues without indicating weakness or giving away power. He never consulted, and therefore, with no one to advise him with frankness, he made mistakes. That's how I see him. And as he consulted less and less, he was consulted less and less, he made more mistakes, and he became very lonely. I suspect that in that loneliness he did foolish things. But I can't tell you what they were. He was never foolish with me. I trusted and admired him, and was willing to sit at his feet, as it were; I didn't challenge him,

79

I wasn't about to become a colleague or a competitor; we got on. And here is the tea.

"Will you pour?" he asked Kate, and she did, with no more than a nod to her more recent self. There were delicate sandwiches, homemade cookies, and thinly sliced lemon. All as it should be. Kate settled back with her tea, lemon, no sugar, and a sandwich, her ease in the role of lady serving increased by her admiration for Mr. Witherspoon.

"I think you have described him exactly right," Kate said. "It fits with every impression I have of him, both the few I've garnered personally and what I've heard. I've known others like that; their loneliness seemed strength, particularly since they had begun their professional lives with great panache, great talents. But somewhere defensiveness set in, and they froze in a mold that left no opening for other views or other advice. And anyone who disagreed with him, or acted from other beliefs, must have seemed threatening and dangerous. It's the more remarkable in that having studied Islam, a totally foreign culture, in his youth, he seemed unwilling to learn anything else new."

"That's about it," Mr. Witherspoon agreed. "I felt sorry for him, to tell you the truth, at the same time that I admired him. I was, for example, wholly courteous to his wife the one time I met her, but I think he knew, from that very politeness, that I had my doubts. That's perhaps putting it too strongly. We talked only of Islamic matters, and I never moved any closer to him; now, I wish that I had. Do you think he committed suicide?"

Kate, who had noticed the pause before the phrase "committed suicide," and understood Mr. Witherspoon's attempt to speak uneuphemistically, answered him with equal frankness. "It's not impossible, but it's very unlikely. He would have had to open the window, straddle a wide outside sill, and then jump or push himself to the edge. This could only have been done on impulse, and he was not an impulsive man."

"How do you know he hadn't been considering it for quite a while?"

"I don't think, do you, he would have died without a note, without arranging for the final stages of his book's publication, or, even more tellingly, that he would have killed himself on the campus of the university where he had so firmly kept his secrets. He would have guessed the questioning and gossip that would follow, and I can't believe he would have chosen that. Do you think it likely?"

"No. Nor do I think him the sort of man to commit suicide, unless he had a fatal disease or something of the sort, and I assume that possibility has been eliminated." Kate nodded. "On the other hand, I have trouble thinking of him as a murderer's victim. He bored and annoyed many people, I understand that, but if that led to murder it would be a common crime."

"Exactly. I think he was pushed, and I think whoever did it hated him for reasons far more visceral than the usual academic disagreements, not that some of those are not visceral enough. I have a much clearer picture of him now, and I'm grateful to you. Are you ever going back to the Crusades?"

"No. I no longer believe in holy wars. You see, some of us old codgers *can* learn." And they went on to chat of other things; Kate had another cup of tea and another sandwich; she was in no hurry to leave Mr. Witherspoon, for whom she had developed, for the complex reasons that do touch us, deep affection. It occurred to her also, as she walked home, that she was probably one of the few people Mr. Witherspoon saw these days who had no interest in his money.

Kate walked home through Central Park, entering it at Seventy-sixth Street on a path that would lead to the Ramble, a wooded, countrylike area. She would have to swerve off this path to avoid it; it had become dangerous, its thick growth and small walkways providing excellent cover for muggers, rapists, and purse snatchers. In her youth its dangers had been incipient, not yet real, giving the place an air of adventure that added to its attractions; the worst, as far as Kate could remember, had been the occasional man exposing himself: leering, inviting, essentially avoidable and harmless. Suddenly, as happened these days, Kate remembered her mother recounting *her* upper-class

New York girlhood, afternoons spent scrambling in the Ramble, the governesses waiting patiently on benches below, talking to each other, keeping an accustomed but not fearful eye on their charges as they popped in and out of the bushes, their voices far more in evidence than their persons. There had been, Kate's mother had said proudly, nostalgically, accusingly, no danger then. As though to blame the "elements" that had taken over "her" park. It was an attitude Kate had, early and late, found despicable.

Kate's ideas and attitudes had never been her mother's, not from the earliest remembered moment. Yet the past returned, and Kate knew what Mr. Witherspoon had also apparently learned, that nostalgia for old times and old values was little more than a yearning that poverty, despair, and desperation might keep themselves decently hidden from those lucky enough to have escaped them.

That was the sort Adams had been: a person not unlike Kate's mother, though younger. Kate had been born when her mother was well past forty, so that there had been a generation missing between them, a generation occupied by Kate's brothers, who were little better than the mother, with less excuse. For had Kate's mother ever really had a chance to understand the system to which she gave such unthinking allegiance?

Kate emerged from the park and continued westward, toward home. The West Side had

83

changed also, becoming the home—or at least the
strolling ground—of swinging singles, where
smart clothing shops of foreign origin pushed out
the old hardware, shoe repair, deli shops. Never
mind, for Kate there was no returning east. It had
a wrapped-in-cellophane aspect that Kate could
not bear.

Returning to a Reedless apartment, Kate fixed
herself a drink and contemplated that day's mail.
She performed this latter task poised over a waste-
basket, dropping the greater part of her mail directly into it. The residue was bills, business
letters, and two mysteriously (because they were
without recognizable return addresses) enticing
letters. Even with all the junk it now entailed,
mail had never quite lost its promise of excite-
ment. It did no good to analyze what one might
be expecting, could possibly be anticipating. Most
news, good and bad, came by telephone these
days. The greater part of Kate's mail was delivered to the university. Nonetheless . . .

The first letter turned out to be from one of the
Adams sons; he had heard about Professor Fansler's task, would be in New York two weeks hence,
and might they meet? Yes, Kate thought grimly,
they might. The second letter was from England
and was more exciting:

"Dear Professor Fansler," Kate read. "This is
going to sound like one of those 'small world'
stories. My daughter is married to an American;

she and her family live in Atlanta, but her husband is this year a visiting professor at your university, and he heard about your investigation. He mentioned it to my daughter, who mentioned it to me in our weekly telephone conversation. I knew Canfield Adams very well at one time (if any one person can be said to know another) and Lizzie, my daughter, suggested that when I come to New York next week I might be willing to talk to you about Adams. She gives you a strong personal recommendation, since she has a close friend who works with you—as I said, a small world. I shall be staying at the address below, and can be reached by telephone. I understand there is a message machine if no one is home. Do let me know if you wish to meet with me.'' The letter was signed ''Penelope Constable.'' Good Lord, Kate thought, the novelist.

She looked at the date on the letter. Penelope Constable must have already arrived. Her letter, mailed in the wonderful English expectation of prompt postal delivery, had no doubt crossed the ocean promptly enough, only to be dillydallied with at the New York post office, where nothing was delivered promptly, apparently as a matter of principle. Kate went to the phone.

She met Penelope, at that woman's request, at the university. ''I would like to see it,'' she had said to Kate on the phone. ''If you don't mind showing me around for a bit, we can go on to dinner af-

terward. I could perfectly well ask my son-in-law
to do the honors, but he would make what you
Americans call a big deal out of it, and somehow
it seemed more natural to ask you. Besides, he
hasn't been here very long.'' Kate, welcoming Penelope into her office, smiled at the recollection
of that conversation, put with perfect English del-
icacy, that had meant: Let's meet on neutral, professional turf. That way, we can size each other
up without having to fumble through domestic,
feminine niceties.

Penelope Constable—or PC, as Kate had come
to think of her, since one of her book jackets mentioned that she was always so called—was exactly
sixty-five years old. Kate had been able to determine that much by a glance at *Who's Who*. The
age had been a surprise, since PC's jacket photos
had been taken by one of those fashionable pho-
tographers of authors, who, by means of an air-
brush or other arcane techniques, give their
subjects the kind of youthfulness skin creams
promise and never deliver. Yet the photographs
had not really lied: there was something essentially youthful about PC, by which Kate meant
something vital, and open, and busy. Her black
hair was no doubt dyed, but she had an air of
being entirely herself that Kate warmed to. PC
entered the room carrying her coat and suit jacket;
she lowered herself into a chair and fanned herself
with a copy of the student newspaper she had
picked up. ''I never get used to how hot Ameri-

cans keep their buildings,'' she said, smiling. ''When we were all freezing in England we used to envy American central heating, but why do they turn it up so high?''

''I don't think they really control it,'' Kate said. ''It's like our economy, our foreign policy, and the stock market—always taking the bit between its teeth and bolting, no one quite knows why. I have managed to keep the heat off in my office by carefully destroying the control so that no one can turn it on. And I keep the window open.''

''I shall be fine in a moment,'' PC said, putting down her newspaper. ''To be perfectly frank, I don't quite know why I'm here; a novelist's fascination with the fact that Adams has been murdered, I'm afraid. He was so dislikable, I find I'm not even disturbed at the news, though I am surprised. Can I be dreadfully ghoulish and ask to see the place where he fell to, perhaps even from?''

''Of course,'' Kate said. ''Would you like a tour now, including the spot where the body was discovered?''

''A woman after my own heart, as I suspected,'' PC said, putting on her jacket. Kate grabbed her coat and they were off.

When they stood, some time later, contemplating the path where Canfield Adams's body had lain, PC looked up at the window of his office with amazement. ''The last person I would have expected to come tumbling down from that height,'' she said, ''no matter what the cause. He was the sort of man who annoys almost everyone, but not enough to cause so dramatic an act, if you know what I mean. You might want to turn him into an ant and tread on him, but you couldn't be bothered shoving him out a window. He was too easy to ignore.''

"You're perfectly right," Kate said. "I hadn't thought of him that way, but, irritating and obtrusive as he could be, he didn't inspire me with thoughts of mayhem. I just wanted to get away from him as fast as possible. But if you went out of your way to meet him, as one assumes you did because you can hardly have been put together on committees, I assume he had some charms I missed.''

"The chief charm he had," PC said, "was that he was nice to me when I thought no man would ever be nice to me again. That's an exaggeration, but not much of one. I really think you ought to know what I can tell you of him, but I think I need a moment or two to collect my courage. Shall we go somewhere for a drink and dinner? If you can suggest a restaurant, I'd be delighted to have you as my guest.''

"Nonsense," Kate said. "My turf, my guest. But do say honestly, would you rather eat out or come home and put your feet up? I'm quite alone these days, with husband traveling. I can offer you drink, a steak—not eaten these days by anyone with cultural clout—salad, and a baked potato. That's about the extent of my cooking. I can also suggest a good restaurant.''

"Home sounds wonderful," PC said. "I want a

loo, a comfortable chair, a whiskey, and an American steak sounds like very heaven. Do all Americans brood about cholesterol night and day?''

''All. They think they have found the secret of living forever. Forever seems to mean golf and bridge games, and the dubious rewards of jogging. I take no part in it. Shall we walk, take the subway, or a taxi?''

''Do you mind a taxi?''

''Not a bit,'' Kate said, hailing one. ''With any luck he will speak at least a hundred words of English, not drive like a lunatic, and have put off drugs and drink till after work.'' The taxi pulled up and Kate ushered PC in.

''You enjoy New York City,'' PC said as they started off. ''I can see that. It's the sort of criticism only a lover indulges in.''

''Of course,'' Kate said. ''New York is not like London, a now-and-then place to many people. You can either not live in New York or not live anyplace else. One is either a lover or hater. Unlike one's attitude to Adams, now that I think of it.''

They smiled at each other, glad to have met, anticipating conversation and community. The taxi driver raced through a red light, pausing to shout obscenities at an old man he had barely avoided. Kate leaned back and rolled her eyes; PC smiled. She had a lovely smile.

Six

If you can meet with Triumph and Disaster
  And treat these two impostors just the same

"TELL me about him," Kate said when they had eaten, talked of many things, and were back in the living room with brandy and a sense of having known each other forever. They had covered every topic from contemporary fiction through the new opportunities of women's friendships and the perhaps concomitant greater impatience of women with stilted men, ending up with the state of England's economy and the extent to which it resembled the two nations of Disraeli's time. With a distinct sense of reluctance Kate brought them back to the issue at hand. How like Adams it was, she pointed out to PC, to force upon them the discussion of a subject as dreary as himself; unfair, because without him they would never have met at all. "How exactly *did* you meet him?" Kate asked.

"It's a rather shameful story, I'm afraid. We were living in Cambridge at that time; let me see, fifteen years ago, as I live and breathe. I hadn't got any notice as a novelist yet—I'm one of your later arrivers. The children were growing up, my husband was involved in his particular brand of physics—that's what he was doing in Cambridge, as a matter of fact—and who should come waltzing into Cambridge but Professor Canfield Adams, visiting fellow. He'd been invited to spend his sabbatical leave there; you know, all the perks, dinner at the high table, and accommodations. I suppose he was rather lonely—many Americans are lonely at Cambridge or Oxford; even Auden was, I understand, when he returned to Christ Church. We met in the most conventional possible way, at a dinner party, he without wife, I, as I often was those days, without husband, and a hostess who would have had fibrillations if the sexes had been unevenly represented at her table. I can't remember who else was there, or even why I went, probably to avoid hanging around the house; anyway, he and I were easily, at least in each other's eyes, the two most interesting people there. He saw me home, and then we seemed to bump into each other, conscious intention on his part, I soon realized, unconscious on mine, or perhaps just the devil at his work. God knows, my hands were idle. We drifted into an affair, my first, as it happens, in a long, long time. Your eyes widen in amazement."

"Do they?" Kate asked. "Sorry; it's the thought of you finding him attractive enough, well, even for long walks."

"You probably only saw him being recalcitrant on committees. Of course, I found out soon enough how recalcitrant he could be. But like most men, when he set himself to be attractive and attentive, he succeeded, with help from one's own damp ego. He did me good, as a matter of fact, for quite a while."

"Then what happened?"

"Oh, several things," PC said. "The beginning and end of those dalliances are always overdetermined, don't you think? For one thing, I met his wife. She taught also, you know, at a different university, political science, and she was totally unsuspecting and a lot nicer than he was. By then I'd got to know him better. Then my husband began to remember he was married to me and not to a black hole and, well, what with one thing and another, Canfield Adams and I drifted apart. I remember now, though, as I talk of it, which I hadn't ever done before, that the beginning of the end came when I did meet him by accident at the market when his wife was with him. She greeted me warmly when we were introduced, and he did such a smooth number in pretending he and I hardly knew each other that I was quite put off. There isn't much more to it than that, except that

92

I can tell you he had his charms, which you might not guess, but he was also basically an untrusting, unloving man. I said today I was surprised that someone would want to kill him, but I take that back. I was ready to dump or be dumped when he decided to cool toward me, but if I hadn't been I can imagine I might have been rather angry, even revengeful. Can any of this help?''

"Oh, it does. The problem is," Kate sighed, "the new young wife alters the situation considerably. I mean, he isn't likely to have dallied in quite the same way recently."

"Surely you don't think he was killed by an angry woman. I mean, he must have been getting on; I know, we all are, but who would kill for love and fury over us; certainly not over Adams, don't you really think? I'll tell you something probably more significant about him."

"Do," Kate said. "I gather you knew him when he was about to be off with the old wife and on with the new. Or were you well before that?"

"Well before, I should have thought," PC said. "Anyway, what I was going to tell you is that I met one of Adams's sons in Cambridge; he'd come over with his mother, and I got the distinct impression that he did not care for Dad. I saw them all later, you see; somehow, my husband and I offered to take them on a sort of tour, and we spent the day together. Long days are indicative."

"Did you call him 'Adams'?"

"No. That's how I think of him now, talking to

you about someone dead. I called him 'Canfield.' ''

"Go on about the long day."

"I can't remember the details. Not even exactly
where we went; *indicative* was the operative word.
The wife—I'm afraid I've forgotten her name, and
the son's too; it was the relationship that seemed
paramount, and of course my husband and I were
trying to mend our relationship under cover of this
party—the wife was being nice. I don't mean
making an effort; she *was* nice. But she had tolerance and an air of determination not to be irri-
tated by anything whatever. The son was clearly
annoyed at Dad, and absorbed in his own
thoughts. When I said 'indicative' that was all I
meant, you see, except that if I were you I'd talk
to the son."

"I'm about to," Kate said. "Not that I'm sure
I've got the same one you had; time will tell. Why
do I have such a fatal sense of knowing Adams
better and better and getting nowhere?"

"I should think you would have developed the
necessary patience by now," PC said. "You're
involved, after all, in what some German youth
group called 'the long march through institutions.' It's a slower revolution but with better results, in my opinion; I've just muddled along in
my individual, cowardly way."

"How does your daughter like spending a year
in New York?"

"She quite likes it; it's an interesting change

from Atlanta. She'd be very happy to meet you, by the way. Would you be able to bear a dinner party, if I promise you the sexes will not be equal? Perhaps I should ask the Adams son and kill two birds with one stone, as the hideous cliché goes.''

Kate said she would love to meet PC's daughter, but that she ought probably to meet the Adams son *à deux*. PC agreed, and they returned by a circuitous route to the discussion of England as two nations under the redoubtable, and in their view regrettable, Margaret Thatcher.

The long march through institutions. Kate thought of the phrase quite often in the days that followed. The weather did its usual New York caper of freezing for three days and then bringing false promises of spring. Kate, who liked winter and found spring the most depressing season of the year, was happy when the cold kept the students inside, hurrying from one building to another, but was gloomy and irritable as the sun shone and they perched on every available step or piece of grass, leaving their litter and often their belongings behind them.

She got into the habit of dropping in on the security office when Butler was there, asking him questions and slowly getting a feel for how the security of this large university was managed. The answer was, though Butler never said it or even hinted it, poorly. Most of the burglaries, and they were frequent, were inside jobs, engineered by guards with keys. Alcoholism was an enormous problem on the security force: they drank huge quantities of beer, more out of boredom than addiction. Television sets, computers, and other equipment were too often wafted out of buildings in the presence of sleeping guards. Not that Butler mentioned any of this; it emerged as statistics. The interpretation was Kate's.

She grew increasingly fond of Butler. He was a man of set ideas, by which Kate meant that right and wrong had been, for him, cataloged long since. There were venial and mortal sins, to be sure; the mortal sins included homosexuality, for which he thought AIDS God's righteous punishment. He was careful not to express racist views, though he clearly held them; he did not, however, allow them to dictate his actions, which Kate liked. She suspected that one day he might wake up to find, as Hamlet had suggested, that in assuming a virtue he had acquired it. He knew a good deal of poetry by heart, and liked to quote it. It was his view, Kate knew, that literature was not taught by the likes of her, but by those who made you memorize the "great works" and beat you if you failed. His views on gender Kate could only assume: he was too tactful to mention them or, to put it differently, coming to like Kate as she liked him, he assumed her acceptance of most of his prejudices except that against women. Trying, in a letter to Reed, to explain her growing affection for Butler, Kate said that he was narrow-minded, even rigid. Yet he respected the rules they were playing by. She quoted to Reed a remark she had just come across by John Kenneth Galbraith about William F. Buckley: "As for all others," Galbraith had written, "thought is often for me a painful thing. But I've found over the years that if Buckley takes a strong position on any issue, I can take the opposite position without any tedious cerebration and know that I won't be wrong." Buckley was Galbraith's neighbor and friend, as Butler was hers.

From all these meetings, Kate learned the ease, if one put one's mind to it, of getting in and out of locked buildings. She had even, in an experiment she had decided not to relate to anyone but Reed, forced open from the outside a ground-floor window in Levy Hall, six feet above the ground and reached by edging oneself along a parapet; she had crawled into the ground-floor room. Since the room was locked and she could not relock it without a key, she had crawled out the window again. No one had noticed her (it was after dark) except two young men who simply waved agreeably after asking if they could help. Discovering how someone had entered Levy Hall that Saturday night, whether with Adams or by such a means as Kate had tried, might hold its own interest, but its possibility could now be taken for granted.

The last time Kate had seen Butler, they talked of A. E. Housman, whom Butler could quote by the yard; Kate had the mixed pleasure and pain of telling him that Housman had been homosexual.

97

"Impossible," Butler had said. "He was a Latin professor at Cambridge." Kate forbore from mentioning all those "lads." The point Kate tried to make was that his homosexuality did not make his poetry or his classicism less appealing for Butler. "He must have suffered," was all Butler would say. Kate had managed, in the course of this conversation, to steal the key to Levy Hall off the rack in the front security office right under the eyes of the guard on duty there. She returned it soon after by the same technique. True, because of her new relationship with Butler, she had been permitted inside the security office, which usually allowed visitors no nearer than the open window behind which the guard on duty sat. The fact remained that if Kate had got in and nabbed the key, others, particularly other officers of the university, might have done the same.

Late one afternoon in the following week Kate met the Adams son, Lawrence Adams, in her office. She early determined that he was, in fact, the son who had visited Cambridge with his mother and gone on a tour with his father, Penelope Constable, and her husband. His older brother, Andrew Adams, had been somewhere in his medical career and unable to travel to England. "We have similar attitudes toward our father, however, so it probably doesn't matter too much from your point of view which of us it was. We both thought the old boy an ultraconservative bigot, and still do, or did until his death." Kate requested him to elaborate on this statement; he did so willingly.

"My brother and I are two years apart. We were children of the sixties—that is, we had just finished college when the seventies began; we took very seriously the riots about Vietnam, Kent State, all of that. My father was unalterably opposed. He became what I guess is today called a neoconservative. Like Alan Bloom, with whom he had everything in common except my father's fascination with women as sex objects, he was traumatized by those anti-Vietnam events. My brother and I were also, but in the opposite direction. It became impossible to talk with my father. He hated, not the Chicago police who had beat up the protesters at the Democratic convention, but the protesters. He was firmly on the side of Mayor Daley. He didn't talk to my brother and me for several years. Eventually, after the divorce, we tried to mend fences with him, but he didn't make it easy."

"I've met his widow," Kate said.

"Well, then you can guess at the problem. She was obviously after his money and flattering in a way one wouldn't expect to fool anyone, but apparently all old men have the capability of being old fools." Lawrence spoke less with bitterness than resignation.

"Perhaps it is only old conservative men who are so easily fooled," Kate said. "They have had to decide that they are wise, and most other people wrong. Even worse, they have to believe that their wisdom is superior, and that they are incapable of a foolish judgment. This gives them both tenacity in their political positions and vulnerability if caught in widowerhood.''

''Well put,'' Lawrence said, smiling. ''You're making this a lot easier. As it happens, my father had a certain amount of inherited money over which he had discretion, and my brother and I admit to trying to keep him from giving all of that to her. But apart from this sum, which our grandfather should probably have left in trust to us, but didn't—he was in awe of his intellectual son—we were strictly hands-off. I think Cecelia looked on us as a challenge; she had inserted herself into a male hierarchy, though she could never have put it that way. I think it seemed to her that she might snatch the prize from the big males and run off with it, like a sparrow among pigeons. I don't mean she was a feminist; if she knew the word, she probably scorned it. But hers was a tactic against male dominance.''

''What did your wives make of that, yours and Andrew's?''

''To change the simile, they thought she was more like a cuckoo in another bird's nest. How did I get off on birds? Our wives thought she was awful, and she was, particularly to them. They thought her comic, too. I mean she was and is so blatant that you couldn't believe she was unconscious of how awful she sounded and looked.''

"I know what you mean. One might even call it refreshing."

"One might call it damnable, when you have to live with it. I don't mind telling you I'm sorry she has an alibi, though I have to admit she wouldn't have wanted him dead so prematurely from her point of view. Have you any clues, by the way? Any insights, hints, possibilities?"

"I'm working on it," was all Kate would say. "Can you tell me something about your mother? She seems a rather ghostly figure in this whole business; not, as we say in literature departments, foregrounded. The police did, I believe, look into her whereabouts at the time of the defenestration; she was in Madison, Wisconsin."

"That's where she works. She's a rather high-up administrator. She went back for a graduate degree when we boys were almost grown; she did get a teaching job, in political science, but she was offered a deanship before she got tenure, and she turned out to have a flair for administration. A certain number of women do, though too often, my mother tells me, they're isolated, overcautious, and therefore powerless. I think she rather gave up on my father about the time she became a dean. She was hired away some years later by the University of Wisconsin, and has been there ever since. She likes Madison."

"At the time you and she went to England, was she still married to your father?"

"She was just about ready to leave him, though

101

I didn't know it until we'd been in England a while. We didn't go together; we met there, and spent some time together in Cambridge. She was exceedingly nice to my father, in the way women can be to men they don't give a damn about. Look here, Professor Fansler, Kate, I understand I've got to be honest with you, and I know that with-holding information only leads to confusion. But I'm still reluctant to discuss my family, especially my mother.''

"Understandably; I would hate it too. But if one's father was probably murdered, the hierarchy of inhibition shifts, inevitably and forever. Which is not to say that anything uncovered or revealed in an investigation has to become public knowl-edge if it isn't absolutely relevant, and not always then.''

"Thank you. You've given me time to think, always the ultimate in tact. My mother fell in love with another woman while she was still married to my father. Of course my brother and I had to be tolerant—we were that generation, after all—but I think it was a lot bigger shock than either of us was prepared to admit for quite a while. Not that we didn't offer her all support. We have al-ways liked her far more than our father, and still do. The whole question has become a little less fraught with anguish these days, if one doesn't hang out with Phyllis Schlafly or Pat Robertson, but no one can deny that life is easier if one can simply say, even think: My mother is divorced, my mother is married again, my mother is going with a heavyweight boxer from Des Moines.''

"What was your father's reaction?''

"Mixed. He didn't really believe in female homosexuality; without the proper male equipment, what can they possibly *do*? At the same time, it was not easy to be left for a woman, not even another man. My mother let him believe he had left her, but they both knew the truth and so did everyone else. She had no rancor toward him; he always thought he could fool her, and I think she thought he was sort of pitiful. For one thing, he was always having affairs, or at least dalliances, many of them with students, and I think it was a wonderful moment when she realized she didn't give a damn. When she mentioned this she used a more pungent expression; my mother is of the earth, earthy, as well as smart.''

"Do you know the woman your mother lives with, if she does?''

"Oh, yes; we visit them regularly. My mother, being an administrator, has to be very discreet; she and her friend share a house, and everyone is happy to accept that. And my mother can work with men and rather likes them. She's taught me, among other things, that most lesbians are not man haters, even if they prefer not to live with them. Lesbians come in all types and sizes, like everyone else. And, as I hope you noticed, the word *lesbian* has stopped making me nervous; my brother said the same thing. That was a very long

103

speech; do you inspire everyone this way, which is how you finally nail your ultimate suspect?''

"Mostly I do it by asking dull questions about alibis, like 'Where were you on the night of Saturday, November whatever?' ''

"Andy and I, and our wives, were within striking distance and without alibis, I fear. That is, we *could* have done it, within the nicest meaning of the word *could*, though I'm willing to try to persuade you that it was impossible for any of us to have got to the university and back to New Jersey without the others knowing. I do realize we may all be in it together; I can only offer as counter to that suggestion the total unlikeliness of any of us, particularly the women, leaving our children alone in a strange house, lent for the occasion, in New Jersey.''

"What was the occasion?''

"A friend of Andy's offered the house, wanting a house and dog-cum-cat-sitter, and we decided to have a reunion and all spend Thanksgiving with the old man; my brother and I usually alternate. We also contemplated calling on our father's paternal instincts, if any, sometime after Thanksgiving, but fate intervened.''

"Do your wives have names?''

"Oh, dear; sorry about that. Believe me, my referring to them as our wives is not an attempt to deny them personhood, though it certainly sounds that way. I guess I hoped you'd leave them out of it. One can't overcome all one's protective
104

instincts in a few decades. My wife—the woman whose husband I am—is named Katharine, called Kathy, and she is a microbiologist; Andy's wife is named Clemence, called Clem, and she is a psychoanalyst. We each have a child, both girls, less than a year apart.''

"Clemence is an odd name.''

"Isn't it. Clem says it's a family name, but Kathy, who dotes on Ivy Compton-Burnett, says it comes from one of her novels. No reason it can't be both, of course. Kathy and Clem like each other too; I'm afraid we rather resemble one of those dreadful chummy family movies of long ago, radical as we have often thought ourselves.''

Kate was silent. There didn't seem awfully much more to ask, or say. She already had the Adams sons' statements to the police. It might in time turn out to seem productive to visit the four of them, but they were no longer conveniently assembled in New Jersey, and she rather hoped it wouldn't be necessary. There was, however, one last question.

''I take it that you and your brother did get your inheritance?''

"Yes, we did; at least, I assume we will. Our inheritance is in the form of blue-chip stocks, and very welcome they will be. My father had them in a safe-deposit box that has been examined in preparation for the eventual settling of the estate. The only thing Reagan did that I can applaud even on a selfish basis is to have changed the tax system

105

so that all our inheritance won't go in taxes. None of the stuff left to his wife will go in taxes either.''

"Who's the executor of the estate?"

"Andy. Cecelia wanted my father to change it and make her executrix, and it looks as though he was about to.''

"Hard cheese on Cecelia, as Evelyn Waugh would say," Kate observed.

"Not really. The effects are more irritating than practical.''

"Andy because he was the elder?"

"Yes. Old customs hang on, certainly with men like my father. This is one I don't object to.''

And after a certain number of general, gracious remarks and chitchat, Lawrence Adams took his leave. Kate pondered alone.

Seven

If you can bear to hear the truth you've spoken
Twisted by knaves to make a trap for fools

MATTHEW NOBLE, vice president in charge of internal affairs (which meant not faculty, or even students, but finances and administrative structures), had, among his other promises to Kate if she would undertake the investigation of Adams's death, assured her that he would gain her access to Harvard University Press, where Adams's book was due to be published. He was as good as his word, and Kate found Adams's Harvard editor not only gracious on the telephone but willing to meet with her when he next came to New York. That time, as it happened, followed fast upon the visit of Lawrence, the Adams son, and Kate swung from one interview to the other. Whether she was getting anywhere was unclear, but she certainly had the sense of accomplishment that comes from busyness and a full appointment calendar, particularly when these occur on top of one's ordinary professional day, not exactly empty to begin with. Kate agreed to meet the editor for dinner, and set out from the office for that appointment. She had a strong suspicion that the Adams book was pivotal to the case, but was at a loss to say why. Perhaps it derived from the fact that the book, an object, seemed more clear-cut than the murky human relations that had marked most of the other events in Adams's life.

Peter Pettipas turned out to be young, on the way up (all editors, in Kate's experience, were or were not "on the way up"; the signs were as unidentifiable as they were unmistakable), and able to classify Kate as worth cultivating for a variety of reasons not unconnected with access to publishable and salable books. In a word, she possessed clout. Meaning, Kate happily assured herself before ordering a martini, that he would probably tell her what she wanted to know. They were in an elegant Japanese restaurant in midtown, one with an upstairs where one removed one's shoes and sat on the floor, one's feet, thank God, in a hole in the floor designed for the women who, in New York, were served in this section of the restaurant always reserved, in Japan, for men. Kate, who liked raw fish no more than the subservience of the Japanese women servers dressed like Geisha girls and given to kneeling before the customers, settled on a tempura that, while not delectable, was also not off-putting. Pettipas ordered sashimi, or some other expensive version of raw fish. They began with a soup that was pronounced delicious by Pettipas, but tasted exactly like dishwater to Kate, who had never, of course, tasted dishwater. Differences of opinion make not only horse races but restaurants. Kate when on the trail was prepared to sacrifice more than eating the wrong food in the wrong position amid sexist attitudes, but not much more. One could not at any rate deny that the Japanese, at least in this place, made good martinis. Kate gracefully accepted another; Peter Pettipas ordered a second glass of soda water. Kate, who liked to divide her life into befores and afters, marked as another watershed when editors gave up drinking. Pettipas spoke about Adams's book.

It was a sound, perhaps a *little* old-fashioned, exploration of the Islamic contribution to the Western Middle Ages. As Kate probably knew, many fields these days were torn between conventional, political history and the more social and interpretative history less of governments than of everybody else. Yes, Kate had heard. Adams was emphatically in the first category, and while there was not anything in his book that could be called new or earthshaking, it was sound, an excellent summary and introduction to the subject.

"In other words," Kate said, abandoning her soup and accepting the suggestion of wine, "boring and unlikely to sell well or to bring prestige if not profits to its publisher. Why then was Harvard doing it?''

Peter Pettipas feared that he had not made himself exactly clear. No reputable press, certainly not Harvard, would publish a book that did not make an important contribution to its field. Certain books were perhaps less theoretical than others, but were no less important for that, didn't Kate agree?

Kate did. She was sorry to have traduced Mr. Pettipas. No doubt the readers' reports were excellent.

Excellent. There had been two of them. Both had, it is true (Mr. Pettipas was being *very* confidential, an attitude made easier by his wise assumption that Kate could easily get access to the readers' reports from Adams's leavings), suggested that a tad more theory, a more evident methodology would have helped the book, but they would in no way oppose its publication.

"Was there a subvention?" Kate asked, beginning on her tempura, washed down with a very nice white wine.

Well, yes, there had been. Surely Kate knew that universities had funds, often from foundations and other sources, to provide subventions for worthy but slightly esoteric books.

"I do know," Kate said. "The Mellon Foundation, for one, has provided such funds. But I was under the impression they were to enable the publication of the books of younger scholars not
110

yet tenured. I didn't know that they were used for
the work of established scholars. Or did Adams
offer the subvention out of his own pocket?''

''No, no,'' Mr. Pettipas said, savoring his raw
fish. The university, or perhaps Adams's department, had provided the subvention. Surely that
was not unusual. Harvard was proud to publish
the book, but no one could expect that the sales
would justify the publication. This was no question of vanity publishing—Kate understood that,
surely.

Kate did. She turned the conversation to questions about Adams's cooperation as an author. No
one knew better than Kate how difficult some authors could be; she had read enough manuscripts
for publishers and known enough editors to speak
confidently on the matter.

''I wouldn't say he was exactly difficult,'' Peter
Pettipas responded, ''but it would not be accurate
to call him undifficult either.'' Adams, in short,
required careful understatement were his attitudes
to be tactfully assessed. Kate was not surprised.
''Adams was, however, remarkably prompt at all
stages of book production; I could hardly complain about that.'' Kate nodded, leaving unmen-
tioned her impression that Pettipas would not have
minded if Adams had been so unprompt as never
to have delivered the final copyedited manuscript
at all.

''Do you edit all the books on Islam?'' Kate
asked. Pettipas explained his special areas as an

editor, from which they went on to discuss Fundamentalism, a subject on which they could argue without feeling that they were letting their teams down. The dinner ended quite happily, with Kate promising to get in touch if she heard of any good books in his area, and Pettipas promising to answer any other questions should Kate find herself needing more answers. Kate returned home to flop into a large armchair and offer warm thanks for decadent Western upholstery.

At Kate's suggestion, Edna Hoskins and she had dinner some weeks later—one of those leisurely dinners between friends in which much ground is covered but there is still the sense, when the dinner is over, that much more could have been said had there been time. Kate had learned to count on Edna for insight into the strange workings of the university administration—not facts about personalities or decisions, but a grasp of how personalities prevailed and decisions were made. In the midst of Kate's current endeavor, Edna served to reassure her that she was not taking part in a mug's game.

"I suppose I shall have to look into the situation of the black students," Kate said, "and perhaps even the Zionist or Palestinian ones. I can't look forward to trying to find out something I don't want to know. Still, one must be a cool-headed detective and pursue the truth at all costs."

"One must," Edna agreed, with a sympathetic smile. "But I don't myself believe that you'll discover anything untoward. My personal hunch is that it will turn out that someone in the family did it or hired a push man for reasons of his or her own. But until that is established, suspicion surrounds us all.''

''I may admit to having pushed him myself as a way to get out of this investigation in a hurry,'' Kate warned.

''You will be disproved in court under cross-examination, and with witnesses swearing you were with them at the relevant time. The truth will out.''

''I wonder. I can't tell you why, Edna, but the whole thing is beginning to look phony to me. Oh, I don't mean just the investigation, but the university and all the far reaches of its bureaucracy. I'm operating within an institution I'm supposed to understand; I've been part of it long enough to understand it, but I more and more have the sense of taking part in someone else's play, as Virginia Woolf so well put it. The question, dear Edna, is: Am I just waking up to how modern life works, beginning to see that it's time someone invented a new plot, as Woolf also said, or are all of us in the university, any university, only puppets or marionettes? Oh, I know, we professors seem to have autonomy, but that's just in the little field they leave us. Presidents of universities these days do nothing but raise money; what are they exchanging for it, besides a name on a building? And what are all those scientists and social scientists doing in exchange for the large grants, federal and other, that support them? And when an important decision is made about where the resources of the university go, who makes it, and why? Don't bother answering; I'm just ruminating to little purpose.''

"Have you read Lewis Thomas?" Edna asked. "He points out that endless committees have tried to figure out who governs academic institutions and how they should do it. More time has been spent on this than on seeking a cure for cancer. He asks: 'Who is really in charge, holding the power? The proper answer is, of course, nobody.' ''

"The proper answer, or the real answer? Maybe committees always avoid the stark truth.''

"Which is?"

"I don't know. By those who have the most power and can control the most money. Or by those who are most afraid of the future.''

"That,'' Edna said, "is either profound or nonsense.''

"Like me who said it,'' Kate remarked. "I alternate. Be a little patient with me, Edna, and answer this: Suppose a certain policy, any kind of policy—academic, financial—to do with governance is made. Who watches to see that it's carried out?''

"Everyone watches. Those who wanted it, to see that it's done; those who didn't want it, to point out the disastrous results. Very little in academia happens in the dark beyond the original decision.''

''I'm sure you're right. I was chosen for this bit of investigation because I knew the territory; I was supposed to make fewer mistakes and jump to fewer wrong conclusions than someone from the outside. But do I know the territory? That's the question. Do I really know how anything works outside my own department or, at best, the faculty in general?''

''The faculty, or some of its members, know everything, I can promise you that. Very little escapes their notice and, usually, their protestations. What has brought on this terrible doubt?''

''Many days of fruitless investigation. I have talked to the members of Adams's department. I have talked to most of his students—he didn't have many. I have seen his university records and know more about his medical plan and his vacation plans than I know of Reed's. I've had dignified pow-wows with various members of the administration, including the president, who gave me fifteen minutes between raising his five-hundred and first and five-hundred and third million. I've talked to the vice president in charge of academic affairs, and the vice president in charge of internal affairs, our own Matthew Noble. I have been reencouraged by the provost. Do you know what I've learned? Nothing. Watch my lips, as they say on television: nothing. Not just nothing about Adams; nothing about anything. Nothing, period. Don't you think that's strange?"

"Not necessarily; to me it suggests that you knew more than you knew you knew."

"Beautifully Socratic, my dear Edna, but doubtful."

"Your problem is that you think there's something to find out. Oh, there are secrets and confidentialities, and you've learned most of them in the course of this investigation. They just don't strike you as very profound. Maybe they aren't, but they're as profound as anything gets around this place. Example: You just told me that you discovered Adams was backing for tenure a young man no one else in the department looked on very favorably. That may not have struck you as the most exciting thing since bottled beer, but not many people outside the department know that, or the stink he made about it for everybody. Whether it has anything to do with his being pushed I can't say, but I think you're suffering from what a feminist has called the onion syndrome: there isn't any center to be found. You don't peel off the leaves until you get to the center, as with an artichoke. You just cut straight through the whole onion, finding concentric circles and a characteristic and rather pungent odor."

"You do me good, Edna. What is it about you that always makes me feel better for having been with you?"

"My motherly presence; surely you've noticed.

My comfortable shape, my lack of sexual competition, my reasonableness. As well as the fact that I'm very smart.''

"I deny I have ever sought or appreciated motherliness.''

"That's because you think of motherliness as like your own mother, or the mothers of your childhood friends. There is something all women like in an older, intelligent, assuaging female creature, and don't let anyone tell you otherwise. Women don't know how to define that comfort, because they find it so rarely, and because the word *comfort* seems to imply mindlessness. But it's comfort most of the world wants from God and Jesus, to name only the deities nearest to hand, and for women real comfort, united with intelligence and power, does not lie with men.''

"You can't be serious, Edna. I refuse to believe it.''

"I am partly. Think about it; you'll eventually see what I mean, even you. How many women older than you are there in your life, or have there ever been, who have real power, whose *minds* you respect, and who are capable of being loved?''

"All right, you're right. A bit right, anyway.'' Kate sipped her wine and smiled at her friend. How would one describe Edna? She was a solid person, not fat, not stout, but, well, stout would have to do to describe her. She was unadorned, capable of being briskly businesslike, no one's fool, no interest in clothes, which in her case consisted entirely of suits, panty hose, and the most comfortable shoes that were still worthy to be called pumps. Her smile lit up her face and most of the room—if that was a cliché, it was one Edna was born to validate. Her reading glasses were attached to a string around her neck to prevent her putting them down and losing them, but they were, in fact, usually pushed up onto her short, straight, gray hair. Kate, looking at her, realized with a start that what she felt for Edna was certainly love; it was friendship, and devotion, and collegiality, but it was also love. And that was an astonishing thing. Could Edna's many children and long marriage, her general air of having long kept an open house for all her children's friends, have something to do with it? Pray not, Kate thought. Intelligent sympathy had to be the prevailing note, and an understanding of power, an ease with power. She is not afraid to exercise control directly, Kate thought. Perhaps it seems like love to me because Edna has no need to be manipulative to try for what she wants.

The next day Kate met with the young black woman who had been first mentioned to her by Humphrey Edgerton that night before Reed went away. Arabella, whose last name was Jordan, came to Kate's office with the air of one adopting the mien of compliance for reasons of her own, but not expecting her airs to fool anyone. Kate had no trouble getting the message. She decided
118

immediately that the danger of seeming a bully was less than the danger of trying to seem understanding. The problem was that there was no comfortable ground on which the two of them could meet. Kate might feel comfortable there, and Arabella Jordan might pretend to feel comfortable, but only one of them would be herself. Angry, Arabella would probably be closer to her real self, which was what Kate wanted to get in touch with.

"Professor Edgerton suggested that I talk to you," Kate began. "He said you understand what it is I'm investigating."

"Humphrey explained it to me. You call me Arabella, I'll call you Kate. OK?"

Kate nodded. There was no question who was going to seem to be in charge of this interview. Kate's hope was to influence the direction from time to time. She knew that she was coming on as an adversary, and that, in a certain sense, she had no choice.

A witness had come forward to say, not to Kate but to one of the administrators, the news passed on to Kate by Matthew Noble, that Arabella had been seen in Levy Hall on the Saturday of Adams's death, seen not with Adams but, as the message had reached Kate, "lurking around the halls." Kate had returned home from her dinner with Edna to receive this news from Noble, and had left messages all over campus on the following day, starting with Humphrey Edgerton, that she wanted to see Arabella around four that afternoon. The student grapevine, as it always could be counted on to do, had functioned admirably. Arabella sat in front of her, looking ready for anything. Which was more than Kate was.

"I'm assuming you know my connection with the investigation into the death of Professor Adams," Kate began.

"I know who you are and what you're doing," Arabella responded, dismissing that opening gambit.

"Yes. It has been noticed that you were in Levy Hall during the Saturday when Professor Adams died. Would you mind telling me why you were there and what you were doing?"

"If I don't tell you I'll have to tell the police," Arabella said. "I get that. Don't know why it took them so long to get on my trail. Plenty of people saw me there that Saturday. I was there most of the day, the afternoon anyway. What was I doing?" she asked herself, before Kate could. "I was working in an office they've given us, seeing folks, planning insurrections and revolutionary activities. Whenever Adams spotted me—we called him Canny, by the way, like you're Kate— he used to really sweat. I mean, I got to him. All of us did. He kept longing for the good old days when only gentlemen attended his university, and everybody *definitely* knew who was running things. We 'colored folk' wouldn't have even been allowed to enter the building the front way. Now that we're inside, he didn't understand why we
120

don't just study and try to make something of our-selves; why are we only interested in making trou-ble? And so on. Do you want me to continue along that line?''

"If you like," Kate said.

That was not the expected response. But Ara-bella decided to continue as though she had re-ceived the correct cue. "Why can't we be satisfied with our remarkable progress and stop asking for more? After all, one generation ago, counting a generation as thirty years, we couldn't even vote in Mississippi and quite a few other places.''

"I don't understand much," Kate said, "but I have grasped that once any oppressed people are no longer 'kept in their place,' they want more and more, even, God help us, equality with the oppressor. All tyrants understand that, whether in Mississippi or South Africa or, regarding women, anywhere; which is why they are so reluctant to give away the first rights. I just need to know in some detail exactly what you were doing on that Saturday, not because I want to argue the history of either blacks or institutions, at least not at this moment, but because I'm stuck with an awful in-vestigation of which, if you want to know, I wish I had never heard.''

"I guess you took on more than you could chew," Arabella said with a certain satisfaction. Kate felt a surge of anger, immediately sup-pressed, not only because anger would get her nowhere and give Arabella a useless edge, but

121

because she was right: Kate *had* taken on more than she could chew, and, she feared, a good deal more than she could swallow.

"Please try to give me a step-by-step account of what you did that day. I will pass on only what is necessary to the investigation. Didn't Humphrey tell you—well, that you could refuse to talk to me?" The trouble is, Kate thought, I either sound servile or bossy; we haven't got a language yet. Or am I exaggerating; would this be the same with any student in the same situation? Kate remembered that Toni Morrison had said somewhere that white women were wholly different from black women, but white and black men were the same.

"I got there at maybe one o'clock, maybe half past. I didn't really notice," Arabella, to Kate's relief, began. "We have a key to the building, and an office we can use. We don't make bombs there or anything, whatever you or the others like you think; we talk, we help each other, and if there's a real issue, we organize. Like getting this university or any other to stop doing business with South Africa. We have demonstrations and like that. Mostly we rap. It's no picnic being black in this lily-white mausoleum, I do assure you. Sometimes we just like to look at each other's black faces."

"And on that Saturday? How many of you came and went?"

"Just a few. Mostly I was there myself, except

when Canny decided to honor me with a visit. He'd got in the habit of that, like the way you can't keep your tongue away from a sore tooth.''

"What did you think of him?''

"I thought he was an idiot; what did *you* think of him?''

"I probably didn't see as much of him as you did,'' Kate said. "From what I did see, I'd say he seemed an idiot to me. Another way of saying we didn't agree on much, if anything.''

"But you didn't have him coming on to you, the way he did to many students, and even giving me the eye as if he didn't know I'd . . . well, he knew.''

"About that particular Saturday . . .'' Kate reminded her.

"It was like most Saturdays. I worked there, because there isn't much room where I live, and I'm not into hanging out at the library, where you run into people and don't get much done. If you want to know, I like to be alone sometimes. Canny stopped in that Saturday—I think because he couldn't really stand the thought of me, of us, having a key to his building. We just made him uncomfortable. Look, if I could help you with some massive revelation about that Saturday, I'd gladly help you. I didn't go to Canny's office, I don't know how long he was in it. We're also on the seventh floor, but not near him, at the other end of the corridor.''

"Was he always alone as far as you could tell?''

"I think so; I heard voices when I went down the hall, but I assumed he was talking on the telephone. He did a lot of talking on the telephone; he was a very busy man. Who he would be talking to on a Saturday, don't ask me. I left, locking our office and the door to the building around five, and I didn't go back until Monday. I didn't give the key to anyone else," she added accusingly, though Kate had said nothing; "I can't tell you anything beyond that. OK? Have you tried asking the fascists in security?"

"As a matter of fact," Kate said, "I have. They hate me because I'm a professor, a woman, neither homophobic nor racist, at least by their standards if not yours; I've tried to get them to be frank with me and I'm trying to get you to be too."

"Spare me the heroics. Look, Kate, take it easy, OK? Humphrey says you're OK, and I'm willing to believe you are. We have trouble talking because you're too delicate and I'm too touchy; I know that, believe it or not. I didn't see anything I'm not telling you. I think Canny Adams was garbage, and I'm not sorry he's dead, but I didn't push him. Come on, do you really think I could get him out that window and over the ledge if he was fighting for his life? I'm not *that* big or that tough. The boys in the administration would love to pin something on me because then they could get me out of this place; I'm a pain to have around;
124

I'm an insurrectionist. So you decide whose ball club you're playing with.''

"Was there anyone else in the building with you that day who might have gone out of the room, wandered around out of your sight, and either returned or not?''

"They'd have to return, because I had to let them out the front door so I could relock it; someone had to go down with them. I was really responsible about that, mostly because I didn't want anybody creeping up on any of us. And, no, nobody left the room long enough to push Canny out the window, and nobody wanted to anyway. We want more black faculty, more black students, more black courses, and less sense that we're supposed to act like Little Orphan Annie. We may wish some folk would expire, just like you, no doubt, but we don't do anything practical about it.''

And with that Kate had to be content. Arabella left with another admonition to "take it easy,'' which had quite the opposite effect on Kate. The trouble was, it was unclear if Arabella could distinguish between condescension from professor to student, older woman to younger, white to black, presumed conservative to presumed radical. Much was unclear. Kate, who disliked undeserved animosity personally directed, and who despised herself for disliking it, found herself cursing the whole damn investigation yet again. But for the investigation, she would not have met Arabella. Despite it all, she was glad to have met Arabella.

She told Humphrey as much when she called him after Arabella's departure. He gallantly offered to stop by her house for a drink and a talk about things. "You sound like you need your hand held," he said.

"I'm sorry it's that obvious," Kate said, "but I do. Arabella makes me feel like I personally fought on the wrong side in the Civil War. I found myself wanting to tell her I'd been to Mississippi in 1964; the little twerp probably wasn't even born yet."

"What you need is a hand *and* a drink," Humphrey said. "I'll be there in half an hour. I'd ask you here, but the baby is not what you need right now."

Eight

*Or watch the things you gave your life to broken,
And stoop and build 'em up with worn-out tools*

KATE had known Humphrey Edgerton a long time; he had married late, and even later become a father, but to her he remained very much the same friend and ally. She had met him before he became a colleague at the same university, met him in the old days of civil rights battles, rage, the birth of feminism in response to the Stokley Carmichael declaration that the only position for women was prone. How she and Humphrey had remained friends Kate never knew, but she liked to think it was because he and she had changed, not in their politics, but in their openness, she to the politics of racism, he to the politics of gender. Kate regretted that she had no black woman friend as close as Humphrey. These women seemed to have condemned her in advance to an eliteness that her presence, apart from her actions, seemed inevitably to bespeak. The interview with Arabella had not increased Kate's happiness on this score.

"Edna likes to quote Mr. Micawber," Kate said, "and so shall I. As Mr. Micawber said: 'Welcome misery, welcome homelessness, welcome hunger, rags, tempest, and beggary! Mutual confidence will sustain us to the end.' No doubt my problem is that I have never known homelessness, hunger, rags, or beggary. I can lay some claim to the other conditions he mentions."

"Come off it, Kate," Humphrey said. "It's not like you to sit around feeling unloved, even if you were unloved, which you aren't. Perhaps we ought to call Reed back."

"It hasn't to do with Reed. I don't know that it has to do with you, either, if I'm frank. It has to do with women, black women, and why they don't like me." As Kate looked at Humphrey she was unhappily aware that, far as any possibility of passion was between them, there was a spark of something that ignited their conversation as that between the black women she knew and herself was never ignited. A sentence from one of Virginia Woolf's letters to her sister planted itself in Kate's mind before she could forbid it entrance. "And I had a visit, long long ago from Tom Eliot, whom I love, or could have loved, had we both been in the prime and not in the sere; how necessary do you think copulation is to friendship?" Woolf and
128

Eliot had been considerably older than Kate and Humphrey. Jesus, Kate thought, I must be going out of my mind.

Humphrey seemed to read her thoughts. "Black women feel very distant from white women unless they can be lovers; there's scorn, a disdain black women feel. If I were you, I'd just live with it. Is that the only problem at the moment?"

"No, it's not," Kate said. "I wouldn't mind beginning with Arabella, bless her little heart, if you can bear it."

"We always want to control the young," Humphrey said. "If we're able to welcome change and not protect ourselves behind a wall of 'old values,' we like the young people we know to be revolutionary; but not too revolutionary, and not revolutionary in a way different from us. I hope I remember this about my son when he's older, but I probably won't. Some feminists called it 'going too far.' Arabella goes too far. She's like a bunch of dry sticks and kindling waiting to ignite. But she has at least grasped that obedience, courtesy, and hard work are not the way to catch the attention of the haves if you're a have-not. Blacks and women both tried that and neither of them found it worked very well. Which is not to say that if I could stuff Arabella into a room and make her get her degree and become a lawyer I wouldn't do it."

"Do you think she really works in that room in Levy Hall?"

"I wish I thought she worked more. She started out with high aspirations and has lowered them year by year. First she was going to be a doctor, then a health specialist, then a lawyer; now she's going to get a degree in child psychology if she graduates at all. And she doesn't really want to deal with children; she should deal with adults. And don't tell me I'm sounding exactly like a white yuppie, I know it."

"What does she do in that room in Levy Hall?"

"She talks to her associates and followers. They stir each other up, try to keep each other from getting into lockstep in search of middle-class success. Keep each other angry. Which they should be, don't get me wrong. Only, like you, dear Kate, I've learned to work through the system, and I've either learned, or convinced myself wrongly, that it is *possible* to work through the system. Arabella wants to change South Africa *now.*"

"So do I. So do you."

"But not by blockading the administration building. Look, there are times when you have to do something to get attention. The whole country, the whole world, your own community, ignores you unless you do. I know that; you know that. We were both part of it. And there are places where that is still necessary. But I think the time has come to work for more blacks—students, teachers, even administrators, God forgive me— in the institution. Whether I'm right or have been coopted is anyone's guess; I don't know the answer. You must ask yourself the same question."

Kate sighed. "Of course I do. I fight inside the system until I'm weary, and I wonder if it wouldn't be more effective to shove, let us say, the provost out of a window. Which brings us nicely back to my so-called investigation. Would you like an omelet?"

"Why don't we go out and get some Mexican food? That's exactly what I feel like. We can begin with margaritas and rub salt from the glasses into our wounds."

Kate ordered shrimp in green sauce, and didn't even try to figure out what Humphrey was eating. In between bites of shrimp she continued to dip taco chips into the guacamole. To no one but Reed would Kate admit that, fond as she was of avocados, she would rather eat a plain half in its skin with a spoon than have it all spiced up. But Kate had learned to keep to herself her passion for plain food, thick soups, and little else.

"Humphrey, sooner or later I have to ask you. Do you think Arabella had anything to do with Adams's fall? By accident, inadvertence, or intention?"

"No. I don't. Her size for one thing."

"He was probably hit on the head first and then pushed out."

"She'd still have to be able to lift and shove his dead weight. You've seen Arabella."

"And you've seen her friends. Come on, Hum-

131

phrey, help me; I don't know what I'll do about it, but I want to know.''

"If I thought Arabella had killed him, or had any hand in killing him, I might not tell you. But I don't think she did, so I'll tell you that. And if I remind you of one of Bertrand Russell's paradoxes, so be it.''

"Arabella could have had help.''

"Look, Kate. She could have. She disliked Adams heartily. So did all the members of her cohort who visited her in that office. He was a notably dislikable man; you've said so yourself. But underneath Arabella's bluster, there's a certain amount of sense. Why kill Adams? She and her group would be the first to be suspected, as indeed they are in any case. His death would not help her. And while gratitude is hardly Arabella's most notable characteristic, it was Adams who insisted on access to the building for her and her friends. She *might* hate him for doing her a favor and for a thousand other reasons, but that hardly adds up to mayhem.''

"Why on earth should Adams do that?''

"I've no idea. But after Adams's death, the police told me that Noble had arranged for it at Adams's specific request; I suppose Nobel told them that. I wasn't consulted, and would have objected if I had been. Giving black students rights other students don't have is simply another form of prejudice.''

"Arabella insists on first names," Kate said,

not too coherently. "All the young insist on first names. It's driving me up the wall and out of sight. Not that I mind being called Kate; I know my name. It's all those students and acquaintances calling themselves Susan and Barbara and Jeannie and Nancy that drive me mad. I get cards, Humphrey, from all over the world, saying 'How are you, hope to see you when I get back,' signed Barbara, and I haven't a clue, not a glimmer, as to which of many Barbaras it is. Or I answer the phone, and someone says 'This is Lizzie.' Whoopy-do. I can't quite find the right tone in which to say 'Lizzie who?' I pray the conversation will reveal her identity, and do you know, there have been times when it never does. Not to mention the times when I have a long powwow thinking I'm talking to one person when I'm talking to another. If someone says she's Lizzie Rappaport, I know where I am. But if I say to Arabella, who at least is the first of the Arabellas, I will give her that, I'll call you Ms. Jordan and you call me Ms. Fansler, she'll write me down as a snob, an elitist, a classist, an ageist, and likely as not call me Kate and insist that I call her Arabella after all."

"Ms. Fansler," Humphrey said. "Unless I'm very mistaken, you don't know what to do next. Is that true?"

"Not exactly. I'm to see a student, from the staff network, who used to be a secretary in Adams's department, and who has a good deal to say about him, all of it bad. She resigned and is

133

now a full-time graduate student. I've also been granted an interview with one of Adams's daughters-in-law, and if I'm lucky, I'll get to see the other son and daughter-in-law. I may even see the delightful widow again, and learn some more financial derring-do. She's going on with her suit against the university; Adams died before she could get her hands on the last cent, and she's not likely to let them forget it. I don't myself see how it can be negligence if a full professor falls out of a window on whatever propulsion, but then I'm not a lawyer, I'm only married to one and related to a hundred others. With all this to anticipate, why should I be in any doubt as to what to do next? I'll listen, and decide that he was killed by a creature from another planet who arrived in a UFO. There probably was a circular mark on the central square where it landed, but we all forgot to look. Are you going to have a Mexican dessert?''

''I'm going to take you home. You need a long talk with Reed on the telephone and a good night's sleep. You must have guessed, being the smartest professor I know, that they only asked you to take on this investigation because they knew it couldn't be solved. Your failure is proof they tried and there is no solution. Then they'll get one of their lawyers to defend them against charges of negligence. You can't win them all, Kate, but I think you can feel good about this case. The police would have pinned it on Arabella, excuse me, Ms. Jordan and friends, but for you. And who knows, maybe another professor would have been dumped out of a window but for you.''

''You're a sweet man, Mr. Edgerton, and you're also right. I need a good night's sleep.''

But Humphrey was not as right as either of them hoped. Someone else was pushed out of a window. Not a professor. Arabella Jordan.

Her body was found in the courtyard of her apartment house at Riverside Drive and 140th Street. Forty-eight hours passed before anyone at the university was notified. The student paper received the news, called in by a classmate of Arabella. They had every intention of printing the story, and did, but not without first notifying the administration in the person of Matthew Noble of the death. Matthew Noble talked to other administrators as soon as he could drag them from the meetings at which all deans and vice presidents and provosts seemed to spend their time. It was perhaps an hour past all these confabulations that they thought of Kate, but they did think of her, which indicated, as she later told Reed, that she had on some level entered their consciousness as an investigator. This placated her ego without in any way soothing her spirit.

This time Kate cared about the victim; she was angry, grief-stricken, and needed to talk almost constantly. Reed said he would come home, offering she never knew what excuse; she needed him, and was relieved to have him back. Kate demanded to be allowed to consult with the police; the demand was granted. No doubt pressure by Reed, with his long stint in the D.A.'s office, had been effective; Kate didn't care whence the pressure. She had been transformed from someone taking on a challenge to someone determined upon justice or at least revenge. Noble did not argue with her, nor did Edna or the provost or anyone else. She and Humphrey, who had also been called, met some hours later; they simply held each other for a time.

Kate was in a state of stunned silence she knew would soon give way to endless verbiage, but for the moment she was bereft of speech. Humphrey led her over to a ledge on the campus, looking down on one of the few green spots in this urban scene.

"I heard from her the day before yesterday," Humphrey said. "She was feeling good, with the old urge to succeed coming back to her. I don't know if this is the right thing to tell you, or whether this is the right time to tell it, but she liked talking to you. She said you were straightforward and not a knee-jerk liberal."

"But I am a knee-jerk liberal," Kate said. "I've never understood what was wrong with that. If someone has a human and humane response faster than other people, does that make them despicable?"

"No. The phrase has to do with people loath to take real action; with folks like the Kennedys, John and Robert, who never really did much for

136

blacks, or women if it comes to that, and who cavorted on a beach that was as restricted and private as any club in the South. Even Lyndon Johnson didn't seat Mississippi's black delegation to the Democratic convention in 1964, as you may or may not remember. I think what Arabella meant was that you weren't all gushy encouragement to her face and a supporter of the 'old values' behind her back; that is, no studying of any culture that didn't have its roots in Plato.''

"We'll never know what Arabella meant, Humphrey," Kate said. "Why did she have to get herself killed? I can't escape the thought that if I had never talked to her, this wouldn't have happened; and you know it too."

"I know that's nonsense. We have to stop confusing grief and blame. Let's try to find out who killed her. You didn't; I didn't. Someone did."

"Well," Kate said, "at least you admit she didn't just tumble out of that window in a moment of irrational exuberance. No doubt someone will suggest something of the sort before too long. What exactly did she say, Humphrey, when she talked to you?"

"She said, if you want to know the exact words, 'I've met your Fansler friend,' with a strong emphasis on *friend,* 'and I think she really wants to know who pushed old Canny. Maybe I can help her. Would that make you happy, Humph?' "

"Her exact words, I take it."

"Her exact words. I'll remember them all my
137

life. Now *you've* got to help *her.* Ranting around is a necessary phase, I recognize that. I've had occasions when all the rage I had bottled up in my life rose to the surface and absolutely flattened me for months. That isn't going to happen to me now, and it isn't going to happen to you. We're going to find out what, or who, killed her. By 'what' I mean what emotion, what source, what organization, what fear; that's as important as who.''

They had met on the campus, where they stood together watching the academic world going about its business, watching in amazement as so many people seemed not to have stopped in their tracks at this tragedy. Most, of course, Kate told herself, had not heard, would never hear that a student had died far uptown, smashed in a cement courtyard. To those who heard, it might be a three-hour wonder. Kate and Humphrey both accurately guessed at the administration's relief that Arabella had not died on campus; but they did not need to say this or anything else to one another. They stood silent with their grief and determination.

But Kate soon had a need to speak that amounted to an obsession; it was Reed who bore the brunt of this, as, he told her, was only right. She knew she was saying the same thing over and over and couldn't stop herself. In between she apologized to Reed, who told her yet again that was what he was there for. She was almost talked out, weary, more determined than ever in her anger when she went to meet the police detectives who had been assigned to the case. They did not object to her presence or her questions. They were white male detectives with no illusions about what the death of a young black woman who was a student at an urban university would mean to her community and to the media. On instructions from higher up, they let Kate join them.

The major facts were easy enough to establish, their similarity to the Adams case calling for even closer examination to verify them. She had died from the fall, from her family's living room on the tenth floor. Apparently, no one else had been in the apartment with her at the time. There were the family fingerprints, but no others. The members of her family all had been somewhere else at the time, and the police were able to verify most of their whereabouts. All of her fellow students, especially those who had used the room in Levy Hall, had been questioned; most had alibis, but none that were unshakable. The Adams family, his widow, others in the university, would be questioned, but no one could even guess who would have wanted to kill her, as opposed to telling her to shut up and get on with her academic work. Suicide could not be eliminated absolutely, although all who knew Arabella denied its possibility. The two detectives were brutally frank with Kate, particularly the younger one.

"We aren't going to find threads from someone's clothes, or mud from their backyard, or cigarette ash. We aren't going to find a fucking thing, begging your pardon, ma'am. My mother watches Angela Lansbury on television, and this is nothing like that. Nothing. Maybe that's 'Murder, She Wrote' or someone wrote who's never been near a corpse in his or her life, but it's nowhere near reality, believe me. We're all assuming her death is connected to the previous one, but that might just be convenient for someone who hated her guts for a different reason. I mean, if I were her black dude and she gave me the gate, I might think this was not a bad way to show her what was what and lay the blame on some fancy white institution. And no, I'm not racist, I'm telling you the truth as I see it, and if you don't like it, you don't have to hang around. Nothing personal.''

Kate had no desire to argue with either of them. She went with them on their interviews; she saw the body in the morgue; she read the lab report. She managed to avoid the media, who, intrigued with the professorial defenestration, smelled blood in a case of a young black ''coed,'' as they persisted in calling her.

Butler was as unhappy as Kate but for different reasons. ''They're going to keep looking at us cross-eyed,'' he said. ''We're supposed to be racist bastards, and throwing a black troublemaker out of the window is just about our style. That's what everybody's thinking, you can count on it. If I could get my hands on the bastard who did this, I'd trade ten years of my life, and that's the truth.''

140

"It's obvious," Kate said to him, as she had repeatedly said to others, as they had all said, "it's obvious that she was killed by Adams's killer. Can there be any doubt of that?"

"As far as I'm concerned," Butler said, "there can be doubt of absolutely everything. Suppose some other student or someone who had it in for her for other reasons was smart enough to figure out this was a good time to get her out of the way? Is that so unlikely?"

Kate shook her head without mentioning that the police had also suggested that possibility. According to plans made before Arabella's death, Kate would soon interview the student who had been a secretary in Adams's department; would there be any different questions now? Kate had the sense that the university had become a figment of all their imaginations, a construction designed to protect them all from the violence of the real world. Which, she told Reed that evening, made as much sense as her theory about the alien from a UFO. "Because," she had added, "there are no aliens. There is only us."

Kate and Reed went to Arabella's funeral, but Kate did not join the police in questioning Arabella's family. She was content, at least for the present, to get that information secondhand.

Nine

If you can make one heap of all your winnings
* And risk it on one turn of pitch-and-toss*
And lose, and start again at your beginnings
* And never breathe a word about your loss*

K ATE had arranged to see Susan Pollikoff, the former secretary of Adams's department, on the day following Arabella's funeral, but a call from Arabella's mother asking to talk with Kate forced her to postpone the Pollikoff appointment. Rather to Kate's relief, Arabella's mother offered to come to Kate's office. Kate would have liked to visit her in her home, to see where Arabella's family lived, but the thought of talking in the room from which Arabella had fallen to her death was too much for Kate and, she supposed, for Mrs. Jordan.

Without having become consciously aware of it, Kate had braced herself for Mrs. Jordan's anger: expected, logical, natural. That Kate should be the object of it was perhaps unfair, but not unreasonable. When, therefore, Mrs. Jordan expressed not rage but sadness, and above all a desire to understand her daughter, Kate was almost physically aware of the adrenaline leaving her body; she had not known how braced she had been for this interview.

Mrs. Jordan was an attractive woman in her early forties. Kate had caught a glimpse of her at the funeral, but Kate had stayed on the edges at the cemetery, and rather far back in the church, fearing both intrusion and the appearance of curiosity. Her grief was profound, and she was grateful for Reed's support, yet felt him even more of an intruder than herself. Why was she an intruder? Had I been her teacher, her adviser, her friend, Kate thought, I would have come in accepted sorrow. As it is, I suspect myself of having caused her death. And Reed, standing beside her, seemed in protecting her to deny that charge. She was grateful, not for the first time, for his wisdom and his willingness to bear her undeserved resentment. Mrs. Jordan, in the front of the church, was more a personification of mourning than an identifiable individual, given Kate's state of mind.

She studied the woman now, even as she was studied herself. As she had been when she met Arabella, Kate was aware that her usual social antennae were unable to operate at their full capacity; something subtle in the environment was askew. Kate again recalled what Toni Morrison had said about black and white women having far less in common than black and white men. But, she found herself thinking, that should not apply to us, more or less of an age and both professional. True, Kate thought, I am not a mother, much less of a dead child, but that has set me aside with white women as well. "I'm glad you came," Kate said spontaneously. "I'm glad to meet you."

"I thought it would be easier here," Mrs. Jordan said. "They gave me some weeks off. I work for a large financial firm; they were kind to offer me all the time I needed, but I think I would rather go back, keep busy. And the work does pile up when I'm absent."

"You must have been very young when Arabella was born," Kate said because she thought it, and because she was trying not to be heavily tactful, not obviously fearful of saying the wrong thing.

"Her mother wasn't even eighteen when Arabella was born. She died from an embolism after a cesarean. The whole thing was wonderfully ironic. She was happily married, to a devoted man—there are not too many of those in the world, let alone the black world—and she was getting the best of medical care. It happens in a certain number of cases. I met Arabella's father when she was a year old; his mother had been caring for her. I'm the only mother she has known, and I loved her very much. So did her father. He's the minister of a church in lower Manhattan." (So the
144

minister who ran the service had been Arabella's father. Kate ought to have known that, but she had not wanted to ask questions of anyone; questions seemed unbearably intrusive.) "We had the rare stable home, a stable marriage, a happy family. But Arabella was never really happy; she was always running counter, wanting to stir things up, angry at us, and the world, and the university; angry about South Africa, and Palestinians, and all the Third World. The tragedy is not only her death but that just recently she seemed to be distilling that anger, keeping what was right in it, but directing it more, not taking the world's evil out on those who loved her or who wanted to help her. Humphrey has helped a good deal. But it's hard to know, especially with the young, how much anger is justified. It's so easy to become complacent. She was just beginning to let us love her."

"I can't think of what to say, Mrs. Jordan. And the joke about that is that I can always think of something to say, but I don't know what in the world to say to you. That I'm so dreadfully sorry seems not only inadequate but obvious and useless."

"We've talked to the police; they tried to be nice. They even sent a woman policeman, not a bit like Cagney or Lacey, but nice. Arabella used to loath 'Cagney and Lacey' as racist, classist, homophobic, and fake. Those were all her words. But I loved it. Sure, they're white, but they're professional women who are friends, who make jokes

145

about men and are ambitious. How much of that has there been on television?"

"The policeman I saw mentioned Angela Lansbury; do you think we are all beginning to think in terms of television series?"

"It's a convenient language when you're stuck. Anyway, the policewoman was nice, and so were the men, though they had to try much harder. What made it awful was that we couldn't help them. We knew so little of her life. She lived in an apartment somewhere with friends, we never even knew where. We would call Humphrey if we absolutely needed her, or were worried. She wouldn't call or come by for months; then she would promise to call or visit in a few days, and wouldn't. I'm sounding as though I resent her, and you may be smart enough to understand that I do, and that I resent her dying. We never had time to get it all straight, not when she was an adult. When she was little, we had the sort of loving relationship they like to put on television but that scarcely exists; it did for us."

"Have you other children?"

"Yes, we have two younger boys." The answer was short, and Kate didn't ask for it to be expanded. That wasn't what Mrs. Jordan had come to talk about. The failure, as she probably saw it, with Arabella would be on her pulses all her life; Kate knew that, and felt that Mrs. Jordan would only want to talk about it if she could do it for Kate's sake.

"What started the anger? Did you ever know?"

"We can only guess, of course. We sent her to a private school here in New York; they gave her a scholarship because they wanted 'minority' children, she was smart, and she came from a 'stable' background. I put these words in quotes,"—and Mrs. Jordan held up both hands and wiggled the first two finger of each—"because I think we all resented the school without exactly knowing why. As though we were serving their purposes; but, we could tell ourselves quite truthfully, they were serving ours. She got a good education, all right, but she resented every minute of it. Being attractive didn't help. She hung out with black boys not from school who reinforced all her anger and who gave her drugs; I was fierce about that, wild with fear and anguish, and I didn't help the situation. Neither did her father, who came on sounding to her ears like the headmistress of her school. We lost her, you see. I'd heard of losing sons; it's a common despair among our friends, but we've usually been able to hold on to our daughters. Not anymore. It's as though by becoming middle-class, professionals, we lost her respect."

"I can't really know," Kate said, "but I think perhaps she was changing just a bit, toward you and the world. Maybe I just want to think that; maybe Humphrey wanted me to think it." (And it hit Kate suddenly that she got on easily with Humphrey, probably because he was like white men, if the nicest of them. It was, Kate hardly

147

knew why, a deeply disturbing thought.) "What did the police suggest? What do they believe?"

"They can't prove it wasn't suicide, though there isn't the smallest evidence for that, and no one who knew her believes it. Her anger was all going out, not in. She was right about that, at least. She was right about the objects of her anger, just not about its relentlessness. But if it wasn't suicide, who and what was it? I thought you might have an idea. I hope, I think from the way we've talked, you'll be honest with me."

"I feel sure she was killed by whoever killed Canfield Adams. She became an unbearable danger to that person. They say if you kill once, it is easier to kill again. Anyway, the murderer used the same method; it would have been easier with Arabella: she was smaller, lighter, and there was no wide, outer sill, no chance of anyone passing below."

"Do you think that's why she wasn't killed in the professor's office? That seems more reasonable, somehow, if anything about this can be called reasonable."

"I agree. But university campuses these days, and especially those in urban, eastern areas, are highly conscious of racism. They are ready to explode at any attack on blacks. To have killed her on the campus would have started a riot. It's still news, because she was a student, but much less so than if she had died here. I think that's the reason. How the murderer got to her in your living

148

room—well, that I can't even conjecture about. The murderer is clever.''

''Isn't it possible someone tried to buy her off, or persuade her about something, and they fought?''

''That's the other script. That the murderer wasn't the Adams murderer, but someone else involved with Arabella. It's certainly possible, and the police incline toward it, probably because it's the more comfortable position for them. I don't buy it, but I could be wrong. In this case, I don't seem to be anything else.''

''Don't get discouraged; Humphrey says you are doing your best, and always do.'' The woman's eyes filled with tears, and so did Kate's. They sat there, in Kate's office, both crying and wiping their faces before they finished the conversation. Later, Kate was to recall the scene as remarkable, but at the time she simply went on with the conversation.

''I have to ask you, Mrs. Jordan, as no doubt the police have, if Arabella had any special friends, any circle or group she moved in that you know of and we may not?''

''I prefer Ms., actually. The firm uses it regularly now, and I like it. Whose business is it if we're married; you can't tell with men, who all just use Mr. I don't know of any groups, except the one at the university. Humphrey told me about them; Arry didn't. Sometimes she saw the boys from her high school years, but she never talked about them; I didn't approve. I shouldn't have shown it so clearly. But what's the good of wishing one had been different? I did my best, I know that. I loved her so much.''

Kate wanted to put her arms around the woman; that was impossible, of course, for many reasons. Kate's impulse was unusual, and she knew the reason for that, at least. Both Ms. Jordan and Ms. Fansler understood the anger Arabella had felt and lived. They knew it in their guts, because they were women, and, for Ms. Jordan, because she was black. They had both chosen not to live with the anger as a daily, hourly throbbing. Yet they had respect, admiration, and, however grudgingly, envy for those like Arabella, who had not reined her anger in, nor modified it to please the world's liberal, right-feeling people. Kate knew, moreover, as her companion doubtless knew, that the reasonable ones, sitting here together in Kate's office, were allowed to fight their fight in a reasonable manner, in a cordial way most of the time, because the really angry ones occupied the margin and left the sensible center to the Kate Fanslers and Ms. Jordans of the world; the Arabellas made their job easier.

''I don't know your first name,'' Kate said. ''Mine's Kate.''

''Paula. Arabella could never understand how she could have been given such an 'icky' name. She swore her classmates thought it a typically black name. Her mother gave it to her; she thought
150

it beautiful. I always called her Arry, but her father called her Arabella.'' It was the nearest Paula had yet come to blaming her husband. "What are you going to do next?'' Paula asked.

"Go on talking to people. Thinking. Trying to guess. I've never thought of working out problems, detection, as only the gathering of clues, or even facts, important as those are. Whatever happened is a story; it's a narrative, and my job is to try to find out what that story is. That's what I'm going to try to do, mostly by talking to people. Professor Adams's secretary comes next. I hope I can talk to you again.''

"I'll be back on my job. But call at night if you need me for anything, or at work. Here's my card. I've written my home number on the back. If I don't talk too much the moment you reach me at home, it may be because I don't want to upset my husband; but I'll get back to you.''

"He blames me?'' Kate asked.

"You, and the university, and the gangs, and drugs, and everyone who wouldn't live a decent, middle-class life once they're given a chance.''

"He doesn't understand anger,'' Kate ventured.

Paula Jordan took Kate's hand. "No one's but his own,'' she said sadly.

Kate met Adams's ex-secretary the next day at lunch. Kate had invited her out, wanting for herself a different ambience and hoping that Susan Pollikoff would be glad of a meal rather than anorexic and picking at her food as though it were poison.

Ms. Pollikoff's cheerful greeting at the restaurant allayed Kate's fears: she was pleasingly plump, a phrase that Kate, despite her own slimness, cherished from an earlier time; a thoroughly cheerful person ready to enjoy whatever pleasures life offered. She was also, it soon became clear, highly intelligent. After they had ordered, Kate asked about Ms. Pollikoff's decision to leave the job in Adams's department.

"Call me Susan," Ms. Pollikoff inevitably said. "I used to object to male professors who called me Susan while I called them Professor Bumbum, but a woman professor is different. I figure we should all call you women professors Professor to make a point about your being here. Unfortunately, there weren't many women professors on whom to practice this sensible decision. Now there's you and several more."

"I take it Professor Adams wasn't overwhelmingly appealing?"

"My God; he had the most underwhelming appeal I've ever seen in a pompous male, and I've seen plenty. Ah!" This last was at the arrival of the food. Kate warmed to Susan, who was frankly hungry and began eating.

"The fact is," she said between mouthfuls, "Canny, as we all called him among ourselves because that's what his absolutely awful wife called him, was like something left over from an
152

earlier era that he thought ideal but we thought probably the pits. He flirted with young women, was rude to older ones, wielded what power he had, and he had more than he should have had because he corralled and kept it, with more arrogance than one would have thought possible. In addition he lied whenever it suited him, which was most of the time, and always blamed someone else for his mistakes, which were numerous. I hope you won't think me unfeeling if I say that when we heard of his death—I'd left the department by then and gone back to being a full-time graduate student—we assumed he'd been forced out of the window the way one is forced out of an airplane, by the sheer pressure of dislike everyone had for him. This is very good Mexican food, considering it's not a Mexican restaurant.''

"Were the black students using a room on the same floor while you were still there?''

"Oh, yes, they'd just gotten permission for that, and wasn't old Canny the very picture of Lady Bountiful or whatever the male counterpart of that is. He liked to offer space on the floor as though he were a subcontractor, which he obviously thought he was. He probably disliked them because they were black, but the fact is, he was so rude to everyone he didn't happen to need at that moment that it was hard to distinguish racism from usual plain beastliness. I was horrified to hear about Arabella; I got to know her a little when the black students first got the room on our floor.

153

She had the guts to stir things up, and of course old Canny would rather academia hadn't been stirred since Nicholas Murray Butler began his presidency of Columbia University, which lasted half a century or something. The word around is that you're going to solve the murder of Arabella; I certainly hope you catch the bastard. I would have thought it was Adams if he weren't dead already, or if he would ever venture above Ninety-sixth Street, which is unlikely in the extreme."

Kate concluded that Susan's wonderful line of chatter depended, perhaps excessively, on subordinate clauses beginning with *which*, but she was in no mood to quibble about syntactical niceties. "Could you be more specific about Adams?" Kate asked. "I gather he was far from the salt of the earth, but everyone who talks about him is so overcome with his plain awfulness that they hardly offer any particular examples thereof. Can you think of one or two?"

"I can think of thirty or forty, but let me be selective, which is a talent I am trying to develop. He was a solitary solipsist: he thought he was the only person in the world who mattered, except maybe for the president of the United States. He thought nothing of making us secretaries work late because he didn't give us something until five of five and absolutely had to have it right then. Most of us held the job while attending classes—that's why we worked for such piddling salaries—but he would always find a way to impede, or at least

154

object to, our going to classes about which he certainly knew. He patted behinds; he thought if he asked for something flirtatiously he could hardly be denied. And the damn trouble is it often worked, at least with women students who didn't like to turn him off completely because he had so much power, and who often misunderstood his obscene gestures until they became absolutely unmistakable, at which point they were in danger of being raped, the students I mean. Professor Fansler, we're talking horrible, not just difficult, or on the lunatic fringe, but horrible. I'm frankly surprised no one killed him earlier, if you want to know.''

"What about his wife? Did anyone like her?''

"You've got to be kidding. Sorry, I suppose that's not the way to talk to a professor, but you can't be serious. She thought nothing, nothing, of calling up and saying that Canny was asking some students or some faculty up for some social thing, and would we order all the needfuls *and* come and help her arrange things. I mean, that woman had chutzpah she hadn't even used yet; she made Canny look almost human from time to time, which was not easy, believe me.''

"Do you suppose all secretaries in all departments resent the professors, or most of them, so much?'' Kate asked out of real curiosity. "It's always seemed in our department that there was a certain esprit de corps, but no doubt all professors think that because they want to.''

"Some departments are worse than others, but all have their problems, which is the truth whether or not you want to hear it. I'm sure you're courtesy itself to the staff; I can tell that. But you, I'm sure, have never come into an office full of the likes of us and said, 'There's nobody here.' You've never told someone to give something to 'the girls' to type. You may never have screamed at us as though we made the university rules, but believe me, many have. The funny thing is that almost everything that gets done at this university gets done because members of the staff in each department and office know what's what. The ignorance of the faculty is exceeded only by their impatience. I'm going too far, I know I am, which is my cardinal fault."

"What are you studying?" Kate asked.

"Art history," Susan said, "and please don't ask me about that department. I am trying to close my eyes to the facts of life here, and just get on with my work, a decision that is long overdue, I do assure you." She had not said "which is long overdue"; Kate inwardly cheered. She liked Susan more and more. But she was getting nowhere. Wonderful conversations, grand people, no clues, not even many stories except the same old one about dreary Professor Adams and his worse wife.

"I'll tell you one thing," Susan said when she had started on dessert. "Adams was a finagler. He liked to manipulate people; he prided himself on it. He'd got himself most of what he had by

156

worming his way around among the administration and powerful faculty members for years. I think he finagled himself right out the window, that's what I think.''

''But who was the one or ones he was finagling?''

''That's the main question, which is the one you're going to have to solve. Have you thought about his family? He had children from his first marriage; if I'd been them I would have called a family reunion of which the chief event was throwing papa out the window. You've got a problem, because the victim was so widely disliked. He was probably blown out the window by the pressure of accumulated hate, which is what I said at first, wasn't it?''

''The truth is,'' Kate said, suddenly realizing it to the full, ''except for the first shock of his death, the violence of it, the fact of it, you don't really care that he's been snuffed out, not really care. And neither does anyone else I can find,'' (except, Kate added to herself, the widow, who might have pulled off a few hundred thousand more for her nest egg). ''No one will miss Adams; in fact, his departure is in the nature of a relief, not to put too fine a point on it.''

''I'm afraid so. It might not have been so clear if Arabella hadn't died, but I do miss her, as well as resenting like hell her death. I mean, I keep thinking I'll see her along the halls, even if I'm not in the same halls. She was part of the landscape, and she still should be. Arabella belonged where she was; she mattered; people cared.''

''Which,'' Kate said, ''made her murder the biggest mistake, perhaps the only mistake, Adams's murderer made. I'd rather never have known who killed Adams if the price was the death of Arabella.''

''But,'' Kate said to Reed that night, ''suppose Adams's death was the price of Arabella's? Suppose Arabella was the intended victim all the time?''

''It would be cute on the telly, I'll give you that,'' Reed said. ''But think a moment. A young black woman falls to her death on 140th Street. How much attention would that get? You know and I know that black gangs kill each other at a great rate, and no one even notices until they bulge outside their territory and kill some white person in a 'nice' part of town. This goes for any town: New York, Los Angeles, Chicago, New Haven— how many cities do you think I could name if I kept going?''

''I get the point. But don't you think there was some connection between Adams and Arabella?''

''My dear, they were on the same floor in the same university and on opposite sides of just about any social issue around today. That's not exactly a connection, but it doesn't suggest pure chance either. The obvious conclusion is that Arabella saw the murderer.''

158

"Obviously. But why not mention it? Or, if she kept it to herself, why mention it eventually? I mean there's a matter of months between murders."

"You can't know there's a connection in their deaths, only in their lives. Lives are much more complicated than they make them on television."

"Reed, will you stop mentioning television? I can't understand why it keeps coming up. You don't watch it, I don't watch it, why the hell are we discussing it?"

"Because it shapes our lives. It suggests possibilities to us; in your immortal words, it suggests stories. On television everything that happens is connected; it's got to be. In life, marvelously unconnected things keep happening in the same prime time series."

"Thank you for those words of wisdom, O sage!"

"You always get petulant, my love, when you feel frustrated. I've noticed it often. No doubt it's a general human trait, but you do get frustrated rather quickly, if you don't mind my saying so. You haven't found out anything useful, so you're furious at the world."

"I'm furious at you. Really, Reed, you've moved so far from your usual understanding self I'm beginning to think you've taken up with another woman. Television indeed. Just reflect a moment, before you start accusing me of irrational frustration. I've talked to more people than

159

central casting could round up in a month. Deans, provosts, vice presidents, students, women faculty—don't interrupt me, I'm just starting—an English lover of Adams who appears on the face of it to have more taste than to give him the time of day let alone days of dalliance, a wealthy pillar of Waspdom who decided for reasons that are probably true they're so ridiculous to study Islam, a dippy, crafty widow and a frankly unsympathetic son, not to mention Arabella, her mother, and various other I shall, out of the goodness of my heart, fail to enumerate—''

''But, Kate—''

''Don't interrupt; I'm not finished. I may never be finished, so you can leave if you want, quietly vanish, but don't interrupt; I haven't reached my peroration yet. Which is, as Susan Pollikoff would say, that none of this fits together or bears, with the exception of the mise-en-scène, the slightest concatenation. I've been given permission to search a haystack that had been carefully arranged with no needle in it.''

''May I say something?''

''Not unless it's sympathetic and consoling.''

''I'll try. *You* may not remember with the clarity I bring to *my* reminiscences, but you always reach a point in any investigation when you feel exactly like this. It is usually, to add to this evening's admirable collection of clichés, the dark before the dawn. Suddenly you will understand it all, as though you had found the magic word. Why
160

A TRAP FOR FOOLS

not go and sit in Adams's office, if they haven't yet given it to someone else, and meditate? Maybe you've been seeing too many people in your office, and the vibrations are jumbled. Try it.''

"I'm willing to try anything, including killing you. That's neither sympathetic nor consoling.''

"Yes it is; think about it. Then try the daughters-in-law; maybe they united to do in their father-in-law. And you could try the widow again. She certainly inspired you with a certain je ne sais quoi.''

"Are you trying to make me attack you physically?''

"At last," Reed said, "you've guessed it.''

Ten

If you can force your heart and nerve and sinew
To serve your turn long after they are gone,
And so hold on when there is nothing in you
Except the Will which says to them: "Hold on!"

KATE woke the next morning to find Reed gone; with her breakfast, which he had fixed for her, was a note. "My darling: all I can think of in the way of counsel is advice from a long-ago movie (not television) with, I think, Danny Kaye. Was he a jester, like you and me? Some wonderful woman sidled up to him to offer advice on their plan to poison the king: 'The vessel with the pestle has the pellet with the poison; the chalice from the palace has the brew that is true.' Sometime later, as always happens, the advice had to change: 'They've broken the vessel with the pestle and replaced it with a flagon with the figure of a dragon on it. Now the pellet with the poison's in the chalice from the palace and the flagon with the dragon has the brew that is true.' I may not

162

have this altogether word for word, but I'm sure you get the message. With my love.''

Kate, when she had digested this message and all the good news in *The New York Times,* decided to review her facts. It's not the facts, it's the narrative they're arranged to tell, she reminded herself. Were there any new facts not paraded out last night for Reed's delectation? A few: for one, she had read Adams's book, or anyway had read at it, and decided that it certainly told her more about the Arab culture than she had ever known, but that only went to show that it might not be quite as informative to someone who already had a certain knowledge of the subject. The book certainly left her with the impression that the Arabs were the single greatest influence on world culture at that time, which was probably true but you couldn't prove it by Kate.

For another fact, she had inquired into the history of the young man in the department whom Adams had been pushing for promotion. For this information she went to the dean of arts and sciences, who had been helpful to Kate once or twice before murder had come to muddy their conversations. He told her, after the usual cautions about confidentiality and the sacredness of the internal affairs of departments and the whole promotion process, that this young man's promotion—his name was Jonathan Shapiro—had caused the biggest brouhaha in a department that never settled anything without a struggle that made the Cru-

sades look like a ten-day cruise. What it came
down to was that the young man was competent
enough, had published, done his services as a cit-
izen, committee member, and runner of tedious
programs, and was good as a teacher. The problem was that his field was Islam, and the others,
whose fields were other parts of the Middle or
Near East, thought that Islam already had more
than its share of the department's resources. In the
end the administration had agreed with the department and had refused the young man's promotion. It happened, however, that the department
had been given a remarkable collection of Arabic
books and documents that, added to the university's already large Near Eastern library, called for
an expert full-time librarian. Adams's young man
had been offered, and had accepted, this job. Kate
had, in fact, trotted around to have a word with
him, and he seemed scholarly and in every way
suited to his work.

Any more new facts? Only one more, which
was more a lack of fact than a fact. Edna had told
her that her friend in the psychology department
had reported that no one had answered the ad
about being on campus during the Thanksgiving
break. Kate was not surprised: it would have been
uncharacteristically lucky for such a person both
to exist and to have seen and answered the ad.
Probably no one would ever know what Adams
did on that Saturday.

Kate was just beginning to turn her thoughts to

teaching, planning her classes, and pondering, not for the first time, how teaching was the center of the academic's life, and yet the older the academic, the less teaching was the subject of current debate, both inner and outer. Somehow the demands upon the senior academic, whether political, scholarly, reading, or writing, occupied more time than considerations of how one would present, for example, the dilemma of the Princess of Cleves. Kate could remember her first years of teaching, when what she was going to say in each lecture dominated her every thought and plan. Was she less devoted to teaching? Probably, if absolute truth be told, but absolute truth is, she considered, as rare as it is evasive. With the tremendous emphasis in colleges and universities these days on publication and reputation national and international, teaching and the strange talents it called upon received less attention than lip service. Regretting this, she had nonetheless to admit that even for her, fervent teacher as she had always been, classroom occasions, like her marriage, were more the setting than the immediate concern of her life.

Having reached this elevated conclusion, Kate was making for her study when the phone rang. It was the elder of the two policemen whose information she was, after the second death, allowed to share. ''We've got something,'' he announced to Kate.

"The murderer?" she asked, hope elevating her pulse.

"Maybe. But not identified. Someone has come forward in the black woman's building who saw her with a man on the day she died."

"What took her so long? The witness, I mean."

"Him. He went away to visit his family on the day of the murder, and only heard about our asking for witnesses when he got back. As it happens, he was on the way out with his suitcases when he passed them coming into the elevator as he left it."

"Well, go on," Kate said, "before I die of anticipation."

"It was a man. He, our witness, couldn't see him very clearly; actually, he was shuffling out his suitcases and didn't do more than grunt hello to Arabella. He knew her to say hello to, and hasn't the faintest doubt it was her. The man with her was taller than her, which isn't hard when you consider she wasn't much over five feet. But our guy has the impression he was quite a bit taller. He was wearing a hat, and his collar was turned up, which our guy noticed because it wasn't exactly a cold day. That's all he noticed, except that the man was black."

"Black?" Kate couldn't have sounded more astonished if the detective had said green.

"It was a fast impression, but according to our guy, unmistakable. He admitted that when you see a black guy with a white woman or vice versa,
166

you notice it. His unconscious, as he says, registered the fact that this guy was black.''

''You think this bears out your theory of the murder having nothing to do with Adams's death?'' Kate asked in the most neutral tone she could muster.

''I didn't say that. I'm just giving you the facts, ma'am.''

''For which I'm grateful,'' Kate hastened to assure him.

''We've got a sworn statement, and he's willing to testify under oath. I don't know exactly where this gets us. My partner and I are going to question some more people in that neighborhood, see if anyone saw this guy and maybe recognized him. I'll be in touch.''

Kate had not asked if the detectives thought the man could be Humphrey Edgerton. She didn't even dare to ask if Humphrey Edgerton had an alibi for that time. Not that she believed for one moment that Humphrey had killed Arabella; but suppose he had visited her at her family home for some reason and been seen. They could only tell within several hours when Arabella had died, so once again, as with Adams, only vague alibis could be expected.

With enormous effort Kate forced her thoughts back to the Duc of Nemours and the princess who so unaccountably refused to marry him. Since literature was her life, she felt considerable annoyance with herself for not being able at this particular moment to give her undivided attention to a love affair over four hundred years old. Kate was certain the princess had made the right decision, but her worry about Humphrey, who was palpably contemporary, kept intruding.

When Kate had finished leading a discussion on the Princess of Cleves that went remarkably well (Kate had noticed that classes prepared under less than ideal conditions often surprised one by being particularly vibrant), she returned to her office to talk with Clemence Anthony, the wife of Andrew Adams, the son Kate had not met. Dr. Anthony, a psychoanalyst, had kept her own name, thus gaining Kate's approval while adding to the ever growing cast of characters. I must stop thinking of this as a drama, Kate told herself, television, cinema, or theater. This is not drama; fiction perhaps, but not drama.

This conclusion was sorely tried by the appearance and conversation of Dr. Clemence Anthony. Kate hardly knew what she had expected, but certainly not an authoritative Freudian who had a moment between meetings of a conference or committee and clearly considered Kate of insufficient importance to occupy one of her few free moments. Kate rarely took an instant dislike to a woman, a dislike based not on wildly differing views—as with Cecelia Adams, for example—but on pure chemical reaction. When you put oil and vinegar together they rush to opposite ends of the jar; Kate felt the same inclination in this room, nor did she cherish the assumption that she had been assigned the role of oil. Dr. Anthony spoke before Kate could.

"I wonder if you understand the principles of acting out," she began. "We all have murderous fantasies; fortunately, the superego interferes with our wishes in these matters. Probably all fathers at some time or other desire their daughters, consciously or not; few act out these desires."

"More act them out than was formerly believed, or than Freud was willing to admit," Kate said, cursing herself. Little good could come from arguing the scriptures of psychoanalysis with a doctrinaire Freudian. You are acting out, Kate told herself; shut up! The admonition went unhonored. Kate's superego was in serious trouble.

"I didn't come to argue the statistical incidence of incest," Dr. Anthony announced. "I understand you had some questions you wanted to ask me about the death of my father-in-law. I mentioned the question of fantasy because I thought perhaps you would wish to consider it." She offered a smile that Kate found about as convincing as that of an interrogator in a spy movie. There I go again, she said to herself, drama. And I'm not even being fair to this poor woman who has taken the time to see me.

"I think you will find," Dr. Anthony said, "that except for psychotic individuals with delusionary fantasies, acts of murder have their root in childhood events that have been repressed, or

169

that are recalled only as screen memories. My thought was"—and this time her smile was genuine—"that consideration of these facts about the human psyche might make your job more manageable. Frankly, as Larry described it to me, it sounded rather formidable: your job of playing detective, that is."

Her smile may have been friendlier, Kate thought, but her opinion of Kate's psyche was not one Kate cared to dwell on or inquire into. "Would you mind if I asked you a few questions?"

"Not at all," Dr. Anthony said. "That's what I'm here for. I am, however, rather pressed for time . . ."

"I'll try not to dawdle," Kate said, keeping any sarcasm out of her tone only with the greatest effort. Kate took a deep breath.

"I have met Professor Adams's widow, Dr. Anthony," Kate said, having wished, she now recognized, to call this woman Clem, "and I can understand that she could not have been, well, exactly appealing to Adams's sons and their wives."

" 'Not exactly appealing' is nice," Dr. Anthony said. "The understatement of the century. The woman is wholly without superego. She is the strongest argument I know to substantiate Freud's view of the lack of moral development in women. I am even tempted to say she is wholly without mind, if that did not suggest a deficiency of cleverness and cunning, which she certainly possesses.''

"Canny, in fact," Kate said, committing one of her very infrequent puns.

Dr. Anthony smiled again; even better this time. My God, Kate thought, psychoanalyst or not, she's just as nervous as I am. And she's smart enough to have figured out that I'm unlikely to be bowled over by authority and an impressive vocabulary.

"What did you think I'd be like, if you don't mind my asking?" Kate said. "An academic version of the widow? Or perhaps a superannuated Girl Scout? Or did you imagine I was one of those who longed to contrive yet another solution to the mystery of Edwin Drood?''

"Whatever I thought, coming on as 'the bad mother' was probably not the best idea, I do see that. Nonetheless, I am really rather pressed for time.''

Kate sighed, with relief and anticipation. "Tell me, if you will, who you think was likely to have killed Professor Adams. I don't mean the exact person, but the sort of person.''

"You want my professional as opposed to my personal opinion?''

"I'm interested in both, of course.''

"My personal opinion is that none of his family did it. One could make a perfectly logical case for us, any one of us, deciding to tip him out of a window; after all, that woman was going to get every cent of his money before she was through

171

and we can use money as well as the next person. Also, we were nearby, which is additionally suspicious because, in the ordinary course of events, we would have been far enough away to eliminate us as suspects altogether. I'm certain that none of us did it because I know where we all were on that Saturday, and it would have had to be a group effort—well, more than one of us, anyway. And even if one of us could have managed the psychic energy to perform such a deed, none of us could have done it collaboratively. Anyway, we didn't do it. But I'll admit to having contemplated killing the old bastard more than once, preferably by causing a heart attack by making him listen to my analysis of his symptoms. My point, as before, is that contemplation is not acting out.''

''And your professional opinion?''

''It was someone who was fundamentally threatened—cornered, in layman's terms—and acting under extraordinary compulsion. That's my analysis.''

''Does it account for the second murder?''

''Of the young black woman? We only heard of that recently. Obviously, it would cost me to my benefit to tell you that I'm sure that was committed by the same person, the second crime always being more amenable to conscious rationalization than the first. Obviously, if both crimes were by the same person, none of us could have done the second, nor, therefore, the first. But my real opinion is that they were done by different people, the first
172

crime suggesting the second to the second criminal, who was probably psychotic.''

"Can you tell me just a bit about your husband and sister-in-law?" Kate asked. "I haven't met either of them."

"Andy is a lot like Lawrence, whom you've met. They both reacted by similar personality formations to a morally unreliable father and a strong, nurturing mother. Fortunately, the father, though reprehensible, was neither absent nor weak. They are both secure men, which as Freud said about the morality of himself and his six children, is mysterious and difficult to explain. As to Kathy, she is a microbiologist and quite simply a nice, intelligent person. She has as little uncontrolled aggression as anyone I've met."

"Thank you. I don't think there's anything else. And I appreciate your giving me your views of the situation." (Kate had almost said "sharing your views with me," which would have carried a note of irony she wished to disguise. The damn woman might be an unreconstructed Freudian, but she was probably right all the same.)

"Do you believe in penis envy?" Kate heard herself asking.

"Of course," Dr. Anthony said, as though she'd been asked if she believed in the historical Jesus. "That, and the fear of castration, are essential to the structure of the Oedipus complex. I take it you consider Freud's theories to be in need of updating?" Dr. Anthony began to gather up her handbag and briefcase, but she was waiting for an answer.

"I believe," Kate said, rising to see Dr. Anthony out, "that when the Ancients got warnings about their children, they should have seen that infanticide was carried out. Without Paris, about whom Priam was warned, there might have been no excuse for the Trojan war; without Oedipus, Freud might not have had a story on which to hang his complex."

"That's very amusing," Dr. Anthony said. "I'm glad to have had the chance to meet you. I take it you don't believe in infanticide generally."

"Certainly not," Kate said, standing at the door as Dr. Anthony passed through. "But if infanticide is a policy of the culture, I have my own choice of victims."

Dr. Anthony shook Kate's hand, and disappeared down the corridor. Kate, beckoning in a waiting student, had to admit that that had not been one of her better interviews. In fact, she had behaved quite badly. But she was not about to underestimate the value of Dr. Anthony's professional opinion.

When the last student had left, Kate called Edna Hoskins. "I'm just asking about something that I meant to ask right after Adams's death," Kate said, "and then it went out of my mind. What with the Middle East department so happily ensconced in Levy Hall, why are there no Jewish

studies, or Hebrew studies, or whatever they ought
to be called?''

''Where have you been, Kate? The Jews didn't
actually get to the Middle East until after World
War II.''

''Really. I thought they got there with Moses,
or without Moses but at his direction, and the Red
Sea parted or something.''

''As a nation, I mean, of course,'' Edna said.
''Besides, there's a center for Jewish studies at the
university, highly endowed and very notable.''

''I see. Well, forgive my asking, but Professor
Adams's daughter-in-law talking about Freud somehow brought the question to my mind. My methods
of association have always been hard to explain; it's
fortunate I never undertook psychoanalysis.''

''Kate, do you think perhaps you ought to take
a few days off? Fly off and meet Reed, wherever
he is, and just relax.''

''Reed is right here, as it happens, not in this
grubby office, of course, but here in New York. He
keeps chattering about pestles in vessels, so he's
even less help than you are. Not to say you two
aren't the most comforting people in the world.''

But mentioning her grubby office reminded Kate
of Adams's more comfortable office, and of Reed's
suggestion that she go in there and sample the
vibrations. It probably wouldn't help, but she
couldn't see how it would hurt.

Gathering up her papers and other belongings,
Kate locked her office door, which reminded her

that she had better go to security to get the key to Adams's office, if it hadn't already been reassigned to some unsuspecting but delighted professor; offices were at a premium in this urban university.

Butler was glad to see her, or so Kate decided to believe. "Do you know the joke about the Catholic priest and the Lutheran minister?" he asked as Kate dropped into a chair. "The priest met the minister on their way to a train, and the minister convinced the priest there was no hurry because the priest's watch was fast." Here followed a good deal of dialogue, with and without brogue as suited the story. "When they got to the train," Butler concluded, "it had already left. The priest looked at the minister, and pointed out that this was what came of believing in faith over works." Kate laughed, more from exhaustion than humor, mostly from affection for Butler. "And what can I do for you, Professor?" he asked.

"Can I get into Adams's office, or have they already given it over to its next occupant?"

"Not quite yet," Butler said, handing over the key. "You want me to go up there with you and make sure everything's all right?"

"I hope that won't be necessary," she said. "But if I don't return the key in an hour, you might look on the pavement below."

Butler, who did not seem to regard this as even a passable joke, merely grunted as she left.

* * *

Several people looked at Kate as she unlocked the door to Adams's office, but they did not accost her. Entering the office, she immediately crossed over to the window and opened it. The room was stuffy and hot. Had it been that way when Adams entered it the Saturday after Thanksgiving? It was not unlikely; despite the university's constant cries of impoverishment, they always overheated the buildings. She and PC had mentioned it. The heat might have lingered over Thanksgiving and the Friday after, on which Adams's wife left for California and he had not been in his office.

Kate sat down at the desk and looked about her at the rug, the drapes, the books on the shelf, Adams's belongings still in the drawers. She opened one after another of the drawers, finding in them little of interest, nothing she had not seen before. She leaned back in the desk chair and put her feet up on the desk, as she sometimes did in her own office in an attempt to relax. She might have occupied the lounge chair with its own lamp in which, presumably, Adams sat while contemplating university politics or the state of the ancient Islamic world. Kate herself had never found it possible to settle her thoughts and cogitate within the confines of her office. For that, she always went home and put up her feet. But professors differed in this matter. Kate lowered her feet and moved over to the leather lounge chair, one of those that, merely a large chair until one leaned back in it, then extended its foot piece even as the back reclined. Kate leaned back. It was very comfortable. For a moment Kate leaned over the edge of the chair, looking for a button or memo that, had Kate been Angela Lansbury, would have suddenly revealed itself, despite all earlier police searches, caught in the foot piece of the lounger. There was nothing. I shall have to rely on vibrations, Kate thought, smiling at Reed. The flagon with the dragon. Who was the wonderful actress who had played that part?

The banging on the door could be incorporated into Kate's dream for less than a minute. She awoke to find Butler, looking frantic but controlled, letting himself in the office door.

"What's wrong?" Kate asked.

"An hour, you said. It's nearer two."

Kate looked unbelievingly at her watch. "I must have fallen asleep; that's very unlike me; I'm sorry."

"You don't say. I thought they'd gone and killed you in the chair instead of throwing you out the window. Then who would we have found to play detective?"

"I am sorry," Kate said. "Nothing happened at all. I seemed to be looking for a button, and then I fell asleep."

"A button, was it?" Butler said. "At least it wasn't the wee folk. I think you ought to go home."

"I think so too," Kate said, feeling altogether better than she had in many days.

"I'll lock up," Butler said. "And you better give me your key too, the one you got in here
178

with. If you're deciding to make this a home away from home, you'll let the security department know, won't you? Can I count on that? You ought to remember Housman, Professor: *'Eyes the shady night has shut / Cannot see the record cut, / And silence sounds no worse than cheers / After earth has stopped the ears.'* "

"I am remembering Housman, Butler. Different poem, different verse altogether: *'The sound of fight is silent long / That began the ancient wrong; / Long the voice of tears is still / That wept of old the endless ill.'* "

"I think you better go home, Professor."

"Right you are," Kate said, and went.

When she had been home only a few minutes, fixing a martini and waiting for Reed, the phone rang. It was Mr. Witherspoon.

"I've been thinking about your investigation," he said. "It occurred to me that there was another part of Adams's life you ought to know about. A part of it that concerned me to some degree. How would you feel about coming to tea again? Shall we say Friday?"

Kate said Friday. She wondered if Mr. Witherspoon was even lonelier than he had seemed, and if when she had observed that she was the only person he knew with no interest in his money she had been horribly near to the truth. Poor rich Mr. Witherspoon.

Eleven

If you can talk with crowds and keep your virtue,
  Or walk with Kings—nor lose the common touch,
If neither foes nor loving friends can hurt you,
  If all men count with you, but none too much

M R. WITHERSPOON had already arranged for tea when Kate arrived; she found herself glad to see him and pleased that he was so clearly happy to see her. She wondered, this time, who else lived in this large duplex apartment with him, but didn't want to ask and doubted he would mention it. He had not inquired about her living arrangements.

"When you asked me about Professor Adams last time," he said as they waited for the tea, "I told you my whole experience with him. You seem to want to know the sort of man he was, or at least my view of him, and that was what I gave you. But since then I've been thinking more about his death. And my daughter's friend on the faculty told her, and she told me, that a young black woman had been killed, probably in connection with Adams's death. That set me to thinking harder. I know there may be no connection between the deaths, but it was the second death, at any rate, that started me brooding once again about your problem. Ah, here is our tea.''

"Our tea" was as lavish as before, with lovely thin sandwiches, delicate cookies, and finely sliced lemon. Care had been taken. Kate settled back to enjoy herself, beginning with the watercress sandwiches. Mr. Witherspoon seemed to surprise even himself by taking two cookies onto his plate and eating them with something close to relish.

"Tea has always been my favorite meal," he said. "I like cookies. You must be wondering what I could possibly have to say."

"You must have a lot to say," Kate answered him. "But I am having a lovely time no matter what you say." Indeed, Kate felt as though she had fallen through a hole in time and was back in another era, when people were neither pushed out of windows nor killed by stray bullets from drug gangs nor blown up by terrorists. She would not have returned to that era at any price, but a moment now and then, feeling like Alice in Wonderland but at a proper tea party, could be cherished. She took two more sandwiches.

"I told you that I was a 'friend' of the university, which is their word for someone who gives money in ample amounts. I know you knew that, and of course I told you that I had studied with Professor Adams. What it didn't occur to me to mention until the events in the Middle East made me think of it, was that after I met Adams I raised money especially for his department.''

Kate looked her intense interest.

"It seemed an excellent idea at the time. Once I had abandoned the Crusades, which I could hardly encourage financially in any case, I turned to Islam. The bank for which I worked before my retirement''—Kate wondered if all high officers in banks referred to themselves so modestly in retrospect—"had many dealings with Arabs; it seemed natural enough to raise money from these Arabs for a chair in Islamic studies.''

"The one Adams occupied?''

"Exactly. He was its first occupant; there will, of course, be others. I heard from the committee about his replacement recently—they are courteous enough to keep me informed, if not exactly to consult me—and that also reminded me that I hadn't told you of this. But I had assumed you knew about Adams's chair.''

"I knew he held one. I never thought to inquire how it came into being. Many of the older chairs are left over from earlier times when it was possible to endow a chair with what today looks like very little money. The holders of those chairs get the honor, but no additional money. I didn't stop to think that Adams's might have been more recently endowed.''

"We raised over a million for it. It's the easiest money I've raised, as a matter of fact, so of course it was natural for me to go back to them to see if they would make more contributions to the university."

"Them?"

"The Arabs. They have large holdings in this country, and have endowed many universities. It turned out, however, that they had a price. They didn't want any Jews in the department they had given a chair to . . ."

"And subsequently endowed with a library."

"You do know about that then."

"I only just found out. I think I see the rest of the story. The price of all that Islamic money was that there were to be no Jewish studies and no Jewish appointments."

"I'm afraid so. All this was some years ago, of course, and I put it out of my mind. Adams wanted to promote a young man who was Jewish, and the sources of the money objected. Adams, to do him justice, was upset; not to do him too much justice, I think he was more upset at having his candidate turned down than at the reason for it. He got in touch with me, and I was able to convince the sources to allow Shapiro to become the librarian of the large collection they had given. They weren't happy, but they learned to compromise, which is more than most of the people in the Middle East learn to do, or so one would gather these unhappy days." Mr. Witherspoon paused to refill his teacup and take another cookie.

"I was rather upset about all this at the time. Anti-Semitism is not unknown in the circles in which I moved, and still move, and I don't want to sound noble in recounting this. I did feel, however, that the Jews had as great a right to be studied as the Arabs in a university department, and I said as much to the administration. They assured me that there was being set up, at that very time, a center for Jewish studies, and that I need have no fear of its not being very well endowed. So that was the end of that story. I don't really think it has anything to do with Adams's death; the Arabs I know are quite incapable of any such action. Still, my daughter and I talked of it, and she felt convinced I should tell you about all this. I was the more willing to be persuaded since I thought it would be pleasant to see you again."

"It is pleasant," Kate said, her mind whirling about in an attempt to put these new facts in some sort of order. Did they mean anything at all? She thought the administration, who were not likely to shut off a source of generous funds no matter what was going on in the Middle East, had handled the matter well. And Adams, to do him justice, had kept out of the whole thing, except for the Shapiro case, and that had been resolved satisfactorily for all concerned. Arabella had probably been on the side of the PLO, as she was always on the side of the dispossessed, but not even she could have got

184

in the way of some Arab or Israeli plot: the very idea was preposterous. Nice as it was of Mr. Witherspoon to have told her, and pleasant as were his tea and company, Kate couldn't see that the information got her much further. Still, it was certainly worth thinking on.

"I can't imagine that this information will be of much use to you," Mr. Witherspoon said, echoing her thoughts, "but I gather that detection is mostly putting together a great many facts and bits of information, most of which don't fit into the final solution at all, but all of which may be of value."

"That's exactly it," Kate said, deciding to have a cookie after all. "One never knows what will fit in, but one can hardly decide if one hasn't collected as many bits as possible. I wish they could all be collected in as delightful circumstances as this. I imagine," she went on, in order to offer them another topic, "that banking like everything else has changed enormously in recent years. Do you think it has changed for the better?"

Mr. Witherspoon was glad enough to expound on his opinion that banks had for too long been restricted in their activities, and that they ought to be allowed to give investment advice and to take part in other aspects of the financial world. From banking they moved to the stock market, and from there to the selfishness of the younger generation in the corporate world. They both ended feeling that their lives had been, on the whole, nobler than those members of a later generation who wanted to earn two hundred thousand a year by the time they were thirty, and didn't care frightfully about much else. This carried them nicely through their third cups of tea and the graceful end to their afternoon's conversation.

Kate walked once again across the park, this time passing a school soccer game. She remembered playing field hockey in Central Park in much the same way, dashing up and down fields whacking at a ball and being, it seemed in retrospect, constantly slammed in the ankles by hockey sticks. Why had they not worn some protection on their ankles? Kate could not imagine, but she remembered clearly that they had not; only the goalie wore padding on her legs. We were made of tougher stuff in those days, she ridiculously told herself, emerging from the park. Ever since her sleep in Adams's chair she had felt renewed, as though she had reached a turn in the road, and was on her way down the final stretch. "*Home is the hunter, home from the hill, and the sailor home from the sea,*" she said to herself, unlocking her apartment door. Butler has really got me into the throes of minor Victorian poetry, she observed to herself.

Kate went to the phone and called the detectives who had been assigned to the Arabella case. Rather to her surprise they said they would be on their shift for a while yet and she was welcome to come down to the precinct and talk to them if she liked. Back to the hill and the sea, she said, locking the door behind her.

Witherspoon's revelations had not been quite as unexpected as Kate had pretended, either to him or to herself. True, she didn't know quite what she was going to do with Mr. Witherspoon's information, or exactly how it would fit in with her evolving theories, but as the verse from Housman she had quoted to Butler proved (despite the fact that Housman was speaking not of the Middle East but of the Welsh), she had already realized that her overlooking of the Arab-Israel situation as it affected the university was a mistake. How did Mr. Witherspoon change that, apart from reinforcing what she had begun to guess? She put this matter aside, and concentrated, as she approached the precinct, on the questions she would ask the detectives.

Kate had never been to Gracie Mansion, where the mayor lived, but every city office she had ever been in had been housed amidst conditions ranging from indifference to squalor, with most of the balance on the squalor end. The courtrooms were a disgrace, the jury rooms and the rooms reserved for voir dire hearings resembling cells in a rundown prison. Perhaps the federal courts were better, but Kate had not yet made it to a federal jury. She had heard tales of welfare and other centers supposedly run for the benefit of the poor. Even if one did not speak of the very poor, and they ought of course to be spoken of, there was enough squalor and inefficiency and unpleasantness in the city offices to make Kate wonder, whenever she had to deal with them, why she or anyone else continued to live here. Because she would miss it unbearably and could not think of living anywhere else, was the answer, but hardly an adequate one. Marriage had relieved Kate of certain unhappy collisions with the New York City system; Reed had taken over, for example, all the car complications. She had also been appalled to learn from him that those with the wherewithal could hire firms who dealt with the bureaucracy for the purpose of getting car registrations and other matters. Kate had no doubt that these folk did not wait on line. Italian-American friends assured her that New York was getting more like an Italian city daily, and everyone knew what getting business done in Italy was like. All of this was not to mention the schools, the custodians of the schools, the conditions of the school buildings, and on and on.

The police precinct did nothing to assuage these unhappy thoughts. Telling the desk sergeant her errand, Kate wondered again of the possible urgency to the police of one or two murders when they operated under the conditions prevailing here. The arrival of the two detectives fortunately curtailed this downward-spiraling train of thought. They led her off to an interview room, making her feel (television again?) like a reluctant witness or a surly perp.

"I didn't have anything of great importance," she apologized as they sat down around the table. Kate refused a cigarette and coffee. She half expected them to be annoyed with her, but something in their posture made it clear that they had to serve out their shift, and talking to her was no better or worse than anything else they might be doing.

But it was not just lassitude. They also had news. They were going to bring Humphrey Edgerton in for questioning. Helping the police with their inquiries, as they said they would explain it to him.

"What inquiries?" Kate asked, trying to keep her voice calm.

"He hasn't any alibi at all for the time when a black man was seen with Arabella entering the elevator of her family's house."

"That's it; that's the basis of your suspicions?"

"We didn't say suspicions," the younger cop said. "We just want to ask him where he was. I don't know what your questions have turned up," he added, "but ours indicate a certain worry Mr. Edgerton had about what Arabella was up to. Maybe they went to her house to discuss it, and the discussion got a little heated."

"There was once a great actor," Kate said. "He really threw himself into his parts. They say that when he played Othello he blacked himself all over."

189

"Meaning?" the older cop said, chewing on a toothpick.

"Meaning appearing black isn't exactly hard. Did you see Laurence Olivier as Othello? Very black indeed."

"You've got to be kidding."

"No. I think, rather I hope, that you're kidding. The police have been accused of racism pretty steadily. You better watch out or you'll have one of those famous black lawyers, whose names at the moment escape me, on this one, and they'll have my eager help."

"You got a better suggestion?"

"As a matter of fact I have. That's why I asked to see you." Kate paused a moment, and the older cop offered her a toothpick. She took it and rolled it between her fingers. After a bit, she snapped it in two with one hand, as she had seen it done long ago.

"Did you also check Matthew Noble's alibi for that time when the chap was exiting from the elevator with his suitcases?"

"Noble? The administrator? The man who called us in, with whom we've been consulting? Look, lady, don't let's try to settle your university feuds by means of the police department."

"Did you ask where he was?"

"No, we did not."

"Well, I suggest you do before you bring a black professor in for questioning on no more grounds than you've got. Noble has one of those marvelous secretaries. Drop in on her and ask where her boss was at the relevant time. I've no doubt she'll tell you he was at some meeting. Check on the meeting or the people or person he was supposed to be with. If you don't find the smallest slippage, let's go back to discussing Professor Edgerton.''

''You're suggesting Noble did it? Twice?''

''I'm suggesting it's possible. I'm suggesting you check on it. That's what I came to say.''

''You got any personal feelings about this matter? Off the record.''

''Let's just say I don't like being manipulated and made to play the bright female detective for someone who may have underestimated just a bit how bright I can be when aroused. But never mind all that. Just do what I say. Or, if you'd rather not, I'll do it. It would be a pleasure. But I rather thought you guys might like to break such a big and important case. Whatever you two say.''

''And suppose we find he didn't have an alibi. Suppose he left whatever meeting he was supposed to be at; what then?''

''Then, gentlemen, I suggest we meet again and I'll give you my theory. You can give me yours. We'll decide then how to handle it. OK? Thanks for the toothpick.''

And Kate, making what she considered a rather well-timed exit from the interview room and praying she wouldn't fall down the stairs, had to face the fact that she was playing it exactly as she'd

seen it on television. For Kate, following the recommendation of Paula Jordan, had caught a rerun
of "Cagney and Lacey" the other evening while
Reed was at some ceremonial dinner, a fact she
intended to admit to no one, ever.

Kate had to call the provost at home to request
an emergency meeting over the weekend. But his
wife told Kate he was in the office, and when she
called that number she got his secretary, also
working late. Administrators were a hardworking
lot, one could not deny that. She asked the provost, when his secretary had put him on the phone,
not to tell anyone, *anyone*, about her request for
a meeting. She had thought of being more specific, but in the end decided not to be. She said
she would wait for the provost to call back and
tell her when he could see her. Then she put her
feet up and waited for Reed.

Reed came home sometime later and when they
had fixed their drinks and settled themselves in
the living room, Kate told him about it.

"What was Noble's motive?" Reed asked.

"Money. First, money for the university, which
would give him power and a lot of credit in the
bank of favors, and then, if I'm right—and I haven't
a modicum of proof—money for himself. It was
easy enough to siphon off; all you really need is
a lot of computer knowledge and falsified records.
Who's going to check on where a vice president
in charge of internal affairs' expenditures went,
192

especially when they eventuate in tidy and very large gifts to the university?''

"Why would he have asked you to look into this if he was the murderer?"

"That's the rub. Hard as it is for you and me, with our high but in no way exaggerated idea of my abilities to believe, he thought I'd muddy the waters and get the police off his back. And it worked, you know, up to a point. When I talked to the detectives yesterday, they hadn't even checked his alibi for Arabella's murder. He blacked his face for that one; I tell you, Reed, he's a sinister type. I've always said administrators were, but I didn't mean it quite so literally."

"I haven't been married lo these many heavenly years without being able to follow your thought processes, or what masquerade as such. No, I'm not putting you down. Every good investigator in the world, criminal or scholarly, has to take a sudden leap—that is, if he or she is good at what they do. Without it, all you've got is a fact grubber, who is excellent as the right-hand man or woman if you're working for a real police force or D.A.'s office. But in the end, it comes together in your mind or not at all. That's true of detective work, biography, history, and even science, I think. So I'm not sneering, believe me. I just want to know when the whole thing shaped itself in your mind."

"*When* I can't tell you, except that your suggestion about Adams's office helped, I can tell you that. It suddenly came to me that we'd overlooked

193

a very interesting thing about Adams: that he was writing about Arab culture and religion. Oh, I know I had seen his book, heaven help me, and I'd learned he had a chair, and even about the scholarly Dr. Jonathan Shapiro. But it didn't click into place, not until that day in Adams's office and then, interestingly enough, Mr. Witherspoon called, really because he's lonely and wanted to have tea, but also because I think it occurred to him as to me that he'd ignored the Middle East aspect of the whole affair. Do you think I could learn to make thin watercress sandwiches, and we could have a proper tea?''

Reed ignored this. "So you thought, cui bono?''

"Yes I did. Not the Arabs; they had what they wanted, and must have been reasonable enough to let Shapiro be librarian of their collection, or else someone must have brought quite a bit of pressure. I daresay they're somewhat accustomed to the fact that, in the United States at least, Jews have been among the most renowned Arab scholars. The Jews, who were setting up their own center of Jewish studies with their own money, clearly had nothing to gain. Adams certainly gained a lot, but someone had to murder him to prevent him giving the show away. What show? And why?

"When you get a pattern, as you were just saying,'' Kate gestured at Reed, "facts fall into place like a chorus line on cue, and they all start kicking their legs in unison. Adams had clearly got a sub-
194

vention from the university for his sound but hardly exciting book. That's not usual, not for a senior professor. He did get Shapiro that job. He did act on every occasion as though he could call the shots and wasn't afraid that anyone was about to challenge him.''

''You think he knew Noble was siphoning off a good part of the funds?''

''I do. And I think the pressure had got a bit too much for Noble. If you want to know what else I think, I think Noble had me set up for the murderer. OK, maybe the brain is weakening. But I'm willing to bet, though we can never prove it, that a witness, perhaps Noble himself, was going to appear and say he saw me with Adams, argu- ing, on that Saturday. I bollixed that up by having so public an alibi, blessings be forever upon the young lawyer who had to put in billable hours even on Thanksgiving weekend. I shall go on humming Arlo Guthrie songs in pure gratitude for the rest of my life. Remind me to buy a record.''

''Come back to earth, Kate. Why should Noble set you up?''

''He needed someone. I'm not certain it was me and not Arabella or Humphrey, but I think he figured out that a racial element was the last thing he needed at the moment. Everyone quarreled with dear old Canny Adams, but he and I had locked horns more, and more publicly, than most. All the attention would have been on me and off him. He probably would have gallantly offered the resources of the university in my defense. When I spoiled that plan, he simply slipped into involving me, to attract attention away from him, in another way.''

''What about Arabella?''

''We'll never know. Unless he agrees to tell us in some marvelous plea bargaining, or whatever it is the folks down at the D.A.'s office do; you ought to know.''

''I'll ignore that. Probably he knew Arabella saw him on Saturday. But why didn't she say so right away? Do you think she was planning to tell you?''

''I'm afraid she may have taken up Adams's game. It's odd how courageous and foolish people can be on behalf of others. Perhaps she figured she'd blackmail him into more scholarships for blacks, or something else, a black professorship, perhaps. I shall never forgive him for Arabella, which does her one hell of a lot of good.''

''I still don't see the sense in hiring you. But maybe you're right. What do you think Adams was after this time that Noble decided was just too much?''

''Let's hope he tells us. My guess is—''

At that moment the telephone rang. It was the provost. He would see Kate in his office tomorrow morning, Saturday, at ten. She promised to be there, and went to tell Reed.

Reed said, ''It's no good saying be careful, I suppose, or asking to go with you.''

"You can send out a search party when I don't return," Kate smiled at him. "Look under all the windows. But the provost's office is on the ground floor; I checked." Reed did not seem to find this overwhelmingly funny.

Twelve

If you can fill the unforgiving minute
*   With sixty seconds' worth of distance run,*
Yours is the Earth and everything that's in it,
*   And—which is more—you'll be a Man, my son!*

NOR was Kate overwhelmingly surprised to
see Matthew Noble waiting for her as the
bus deposited her at the stop nearest the university; not surprised, but disappointed. She had
overestimated the judgment of the provost. Kate's
opinion of administrators, never high, sank a
notch. She looked around her to see if there was
any sign of Butler; she could see none, but she
felt confidence nonetheless. She would not mention his presence to Noble—Butler had his job to
think of—but it made her defiant manner to Noble
easier to bring off.

She had called Butler the evening before. "You
on duty this Saturday, as always?" she had asked.

"As always," he had said. "You planning to fall asleep anywhere else I've got the key to?"

"Just planning to confront Adams's murderer," Kate said. She told him who it was. "I'll be taking a bus up to talk to the provost about him in the morning. I just thought, if you could see me, even if I couldn't see you . . ."

"Security's got to be everywhere," Butler had said. Kate was pleased to have gotten to know Butler, pleased, as academics often are, to have established a relationship with a working man or woman. Kate didn't delude herself about the permanence of the relationship, or the depth, but she felt good, nonetheless, as when one is welcomed into their home by strangers in a foreign country.

"On the way to see our second in command, I understand," Noble said, as though he had been waiting for her to speak first. "Mind if I walk along with you?"

"Not at all. Provided you don't suggest that we enter any elevators, or in fact go anywhere above the first floor. I'm becoming acrophobic in my old age; how about you?"

"I'm not acrophobic. Suppose you never make it to the provost's office."

"Unfortunate for both of us," Kate said, turning the corner to the street on which the chief administration building stood. "I haven't left a sealed letter with my lawyer to be opened in the event of my death, but I have told my husband all

199

about it, as well as the two detectives assigned to the case.''

"They tried to look at my appointment book last night. I told them to get a search warrant.''

"Unwise. Do you know that in 1980 police in large cities investigated more than a million crimes, but that only about fifteen thousand search warrants were issued? The niceties of the Constitution, especially the fourth amendment, are not always as strictly observed as one might wish.''

"Did you read that fact or just make it up, a habit I suspect many women of indulging in with regard to statistics.''

"I read it in a book some friends of mine are writing on the law; that section was on procedure. Would you like the reference?''

"Let's stop right here, Professor Fansler. I have a gun, and I'm prepared to use it, if only to shoot you in the leg. Gang wars are spreading, as you may have heard.''

"Face it, Mr. Noble. Either you kill me, in which case you will certainly have a full-fledged investigation on your hands, or you wound me, and you'll have me on your hands. I think you better give it up. Unless, of course, you'd like to come with me to the provost's office, for which I am already five minutes late. And the provost was doing me a favor, seeing me on a Saturday; not very grateful of me to be late. Interesting, isn't it, how few people are around the campus on a Saturday, even when it's not a holiday weekend?''

"You're brave, for a woman."

"Actually, I'm not. In absolute contradiction to Freud, I have simply developed a very acute moral sense. And you offend it."

"I know you suspect me; I haven't admitted anything. You've got it all wrong, Professor Fansler."

"Come along with me then to see the provost. You can give him your side of the story. But it might be a good idea to have police officers present, if you've taken to carrying a gun."

"That was just a bluff."

"Good," Kate said. "You've no idea how relieved I am to hear it." And she walked slowly away from him, turning her back, counting on Noble's cowardice and Butler's bravery. And, she added to herself, entering the building and knocking on the provost's door, if that act was even half successful, you really *have* no idea.

The provost rose to meet Kate with a mixture of worry and bonhomie.

"You shouldn't have told Matthew Noble," Kate said. "I asked you not to tell anyone. He's just threatened me with a gun. At least, I hope he hasn't got a gun, and was just pretending."

"I wouldn't have told him," the provost said, "but he happened to drop in last evening, so I mentioned it in the course of things. When you said don't tell anyone, I didn't think you meant my own staff."

"That, unfortunately, is just what I meant,"

AMANDA CROSS

Kate said. "You'd better sit down, this may take quite a while. And when I'm finished, you'd better put an accountant or an actuary to work pretty fast. That is, if you want to know what happened to a fair chunk of university money."

The provost sank into the chair behind his desk. Before Kate began to speak, she had time to observe that probably never, before or since, had she had an administrator's completely undivided attention. She wished it could have been for a more scholarly purpose.

When Kate left the provost's office hours later, she looked somewhat anxiously for Matthew Noble, but he was not to be seen. She decided that if he intended to shoot her, always supposing he had a gun, he would not lack for chances no matter what she did. And if he had some other nefarious plan in mind—well, she intended to stay away from windows in his company. His must have been a nicely developed technique; pressure, perhaps, on the carotid artery or a blow on the side of the head, which would be smashed in the fall, or plastic over the face, and then out the window. Little problem with the light Arabella. But even with Adams, not too difficult, particularly if the blow was unexpected. Kate had taken the opportunity to observe Noble's build with more attention than she had previously taken. He was large, and in excellent shape. Probably practiced on those ma-
202

chines they had now in health clubs; or perhaps he had a black belt. One never knew these days.

Kate was walking toward a new apartment building into which, as she knew, Edna Hoskins had recently moved. She had not called ahead. She didn't know if Edna was home, hadn't decided until she had left the provost's office that she was going to call on Edna. It occurred to her that it was not a terribly sensible thing to do, but she felt propelled and did not question the urgency she felt.

Edna was home, and quite surprised to see Kate.

"Come in and sit down. What a nice surprise. It never occurred to me you might be around these parts on a Saturday. I'll make some coffee."

"Don't bother," Kate said. "Didn't Matthew Noble tell you I might be seen around these parts this Saturday?"

"No," Edna said, looking worried. "What do you mean?"

Kate looked at Edna, who had sat down nervously in an armchair. The apartment was a lovely one, if you liked modern apartments; its large corner living room had windows on all sides, with a pleasing urban view and plenty of sunshine.

"I'd like to see your apartment," Kate said. "You said you'd invite me when you had finished fixing it up; it looks quite finished from here."

"What is it, Kate?" Edna said.

Kate got up and began pacing the room. Edna

203

seemed about to rise also, but Kate stopped her. "Don't get up; just sit and listen. I'm trusting, you see, that you're unarmed and aren't going to attack me, but I'd be grateful if you'd stay where you are; just sit back and listen. No, don't say anything, not yet anyway."

Kate crossed in back of the couch and leaned on it, facing Edna. "You're the part I mind most. Being betrayed or set up by the likes of Noble is upsetting, even threatening, but he never pretended to be a friend. I have a rather old-fashioned idea of friendship, and since it's probably the only old-fashioned thing about me, I hate to see it undermined. I'd never really have taken on this job without your eager encouragement, without your clever warnings about the dangers to Humphrey and Arabella. I suppose when you went on about that you didn't know you'd have to kill her and let Noble try to get Humphrey accused of her murder. Or did you? Tell me, did all this come as a nasty surprise, or was it part of the plan from the beginning?"

Edna tried to answer, but cried instead. She fumbled in her pocket for a handkerchief, but the tears were not to be stemmed.

"Perfect," Kate said. "I never understood before why it annoyed male professionals so much to see a woman crying. I thought it was just because they were out of touch with their feelings and we wonderful females, used to nurturing and intimacy, were not so inhibited. But it's a bit much, don't you think, to cry over two deaths, one of which I shall be mourning until *my* death, when you had a hand in planning both? Or were you merely overcome with womanly surprise when you found out what Noble was up to? I do want an answer, you know, if you can manage to control your sobs.''

"I don't think you do want an answer," Edna managed to say. "You're just angry; I don't blame you."

"That makes me feel better, it really does," Kate said. "Never mind that we were supposed to be friends. That you led me on with a little charade of deception that would make John le Carré's characters look like folks from a nursery rhyme. We women haven't had a lot of professional women friends until rather recently, which may be why I resent this even more.

"I know," Kate continued, "you suspect I'm angry more for my own pride than the deaths, and you're probably right. I'm angry as hell in my pride, and angry a lot deeper down about Arabella. Well, believe it or not, I'm going to stop talking in about two minutes, and I'd like to hear why you helped to set me up for this plot, and I guess I'd also like to know why you cared for me so little that I was worth faking a friendship for. I mean, if I'm that hateable, I'd like to know about it."

"How did you find out?"

"Ever the practical woman," Kate said. "I figured it out; I told you quite a while ago I thought the whole thing was phony, only I didn't know how phony. Oh, I didn't think of you right away; when I expounded the whole pretty plot to Reed I didn't even mention you. Because even though I was sure you had to be in on it, I didn't want to believe it. Sure, you had suggested I plug in to the network of administrative secretaries, not to mention the women faculty: you knew they didn't know anything, that Noble had covered his tracks well. All you could do, after enticing me into this little charade, was to keep suggesting, as subtly as possible, that the family had the biggest motive. Were you going to see one of Adams's sons accused of this? Or had you planned to pin it on the widow, who fouled you up by disappearing to see her sick uncle three thousand miles away?''

''Are you finished?'' Edna asked. She seemed to have stopped crying, but not easily.

''I'm not quite finished. I still didn't want to believe it. There could have been an innocent explanation for all these things. After all, you didn't try to steer me away from Mr. Witherspoon; Noble did. And then, rather late last night, I had a phone call from PC.''

''Who?''

''Penelope Constable, a famous English novelist, turned up by the women's faculty network. That really was cute of you, Edna, pretending to have faith in the sisterhood: I liked that touch. It had me fooled, no question.''

"What did the English novelist say?"

"She said, my dear Edna, that her son-in-law, a professor in the psychology department, had mentioned that your friend had indeed had an answer to the ad. But you had told your friend when she reported it to you that it was no longer needed and to forget about it. You told me there was no answer, remember? Only it seems one young man had been on the campus on that Saturday and might have seen—what? We shall probably find out as this investigation winds its way down. I don't, however, take great delight in the fact that your guilt was finally proved to me by a coincidence: PC's son-in-law happened to be in the office of your friend when the answer to the ad came in, and happened to think of it when PC recounted to him the events of that particular Saturday on Thanksgiving weekend. I had begun to suspect you had lied to me on many occasions, but this was the first *proof* that you had lied to me, and it went a long way to convincing me that you'd been, if you'll forgive my mentioning it, a total shit. And I warn you, if you try to overcome me for any reason, I have a lot of adrenaline surging through my system." With that, Kate, in denial of her last statement, walked around the couch and dropped onto it.

Edna leaned forward and dropped her head into her hands. Kate was now ready to let her speak. It took a while.

Edna said, "I got on to what Matthew Noble

was doing quite by accident. When we set up the center for Jewish studies, I asked to see how the Arab money was used; I wasn't used to dealing with such large endowments. The center for Jewish studies came under my direction, not that it was exactly a professional school, but there'd been some reorganization, and programs and centers were put under my umbrella.

"I didn't ask Matthew about the Arab money; I asked the development office and the controller. I'd learned to read financial statements and actuarial accounts from my husband when I took the job. I thought I ought to know, since I had a friend who got into some trouble because he'd been an academic and had had the wool pulled over his eyes for a while in a similar situation."

"Where is your husband?" Kate suddenly asked. It had not occurred to her to wonder if the husband was home, or in on the scheme, or even a danger.

Edna said, "He's at the hospital getting a radiation treatment. He doesn't know anything about this. He has cancer of the prostate."

"I'm sorry," Kate heard herself saying. "Why didn't you tell me?" The question sounded idiotic to her own ears, but not, it seemed, to Edna's.

"I wanted to. But if I started telling you any of it, I would have come apart. I needed the money. I wanted us to have a nice place to live, and I wanted it now. Not that I would ever have started this. You slip into things. I faced Matthew with what I'd found. I said I had to tell the provost or president unless he would put the money back. He said he wouldn't and that the chances of it being discovered were slim. I realize now that was non-sense, but he'd certainly been safe for quite a while. I suppose I wanted to believe it. Somehow, I started letting him pay me money. It seems in-credible as I tell it; I told myself I'd keep it as evidence, in a separate account, and give it back when he failed to make up the amount he'd stolen. Then Frank got sick and—well, things fell apart."

"Why did Noble have to kill Adams?"

"He'd gone on demanding things. He liked his sense of being able to call the shots, that was the trouble. Matthew began to be afraid. Adams had even insisted on Matthew's giving the black kids a key to Levy Hall, though Matthew managed to do it through Humphrey. Adams knew that would get under Matthew's skin. He didn't know it would mean his own life."

"When did he tell you what he'd done?"

"When he got the idea of asking you to solve the case. He threatened me with exposure. He even said I could be accused as an accomplice in the murder."

"What exactly was I supposed to accomplish? Or not accomplish?"

"You were a diversion. He hoped there'd be publicity and a lot of talk and that the police would get fed up sooner. Believe me, Kate, I tried to talk him out of it. But he said if I didn't talk you
209

AMANDA CROSS

into it I'd go down with him. I knew that was true. And now, of course, I'll go down with him anyway."

"Probably. He'll try to blame you for most of it. Unless someone can strike a bargain with him. Perhaps the provost. But I'm not going to raise a finger, as my mother used to say."

"About Arabella. She'd seen him that Saturday. I think she planned to tell you, but she told him first. She said she'd keep it to herself if he offered her something. Poor Arabella. She wasn't unlike Adams, wanting to manipulate systems that had been entrenched far too long to be that easily diverted from their ends."

"Adams was a finagler," Kate said.

"A what?"

"Susan Pollikoff's word. A finagler. You know, everyone underestimates the resentment of apparently powerless people. And the things they have to say. Noble underestimated it. His other mistake was not to realize that I look for narratives. That's my profession, not being a detective. That's the profession of every professor of literature. He thought to provide a diversion, but lit crit teaches you to be on the watchout for exactly that. We deal in subtexts, in the hidden story."

Edna said, "What are you going to do?"

"About you? I don't know. I've already told the provost about Noble and made sure he called the police. I didn't mention you. So if you have the
210

poison in a vessel with a pestle, now's the time to bring it out. Or a flagon with a dragon.''

But Edna had begun to cry again. In the end, Kate sat on the arm of her chair and patted her shoulder. After a while, Kate left.

''A masterful job, if you don't mind my saying so,'' the provost said some weeks later.

''But I do mind,'' Kate said, accepting a glass of scotch after declining sherry. It was late in the afternoon. ''It was a most womanly job; most men couldn't have done it. But if acting like a man is your highest compliment, then I can only accept it while hoping to change your terms of reference.''

The provost had the grace to smile.

''Thank God Noble's been cooperative, anyway,'' he said. ''We wouldn't press charges; he'll only be tried on the Adams murder, and he'll plead manslaughter. We'll keep all this out of the papers. I can't think it would encourage donors of any faith, do you?'' He didn't exactly wink at Kate, but he didn't exactly not wink either.

''He blackmailed Edna Hoskins,'' Kate said, ''and cost her her job. I think she was very good at it.''

''She was,'' the provost said. ''We're helping her to find another position. Noble is playing his part nobly. I was sorry to hear about her husband.''

''I learned a certain amount about blackmail,''

211

Kate said. "It's dangerous, as when Arabella tried it with Noble, or when Adams went too far. But it worked when Noble tried it with Edna; she felt she had no choice."

"Blackmail is a dreadful business," the provost said with, Kate thought but she might have imagined it, a suspicion of nervousness.

"Dreadful," Kate said. "But this whole investigation has revealed nothing but dreadful things. Of which by far the worst, in my opinion, was the death of Arabella Jordan."

"Of course. We all feel that."

"But some of us," Kate said, "feel it more guiltily, or more profoundly, than others. I do."

"But what can be done?" the provost said. "We have written to her family; the president has written. I understand her father cherishes the letter."

"I'm sure he does. And I'm sure her mother cherishes Arabella's father's cherishing it. It has no doubt made him easier to live with." Kate examined her briefcase with a thoughtfulness that utilitarian object seemed hardly to deserve.

The provost said, "What do you want?"

"I'm not pretending it isn't blackmail," Kate said. "I detest pretensions; always have. It's blackmail."

"I repeat my question," the provost said, not kindly.

"I thought three large scholarships," Kate said. "Generous, you know, covering living expenses, and what the student would have been able to offer
212

toward her or his family's support had she or he not gone to college. I was rather hoping for shes, of course, but it doesn't pay to be sexist. They'll be the Arabella Jordan Fellowships, of course. I rather hope they'll come to be called the Arries."

"You'd better settle for one or two," the provost said.

"Three," Kate said. "It's a holy number."

She got up then and left before the provost could answer her. Kate had little doubt that thought of this story reaching the wealthier Arab and Jewish communities, not to mention the considerably poorer black communities, was going to be sufficient inspiration to the provost in the raising of the necessary funds.

It was too bad, really, about the provost. Kate had always rather admired him, as much as she could admire any administrator. They were unlikely to meet, except under the most formal circumstances, ever again.

Kate passed Levy Hall on her way off the campus and into her beloved city streets. Even the garbage and graffiti looked better than they had in a long, long time.

WRITING A WOMAN'S LIFE
by Carolyn G. Heilbrun, "Amanda Cross"

With subtlety and eloquence, Carolyn Heilbrun shows how those who write about women's lives, biographers *and* autobiographers, have suppressed the truth of the female experience, in order to make the "written life" conform to society's expectations of what that life should be.

Drawing on the experiences of celebrated women, from George Sand to Virginia Woolf to Dorothy Sayers, Heilbrun examines the struggle these writers undertook when it became impossible for them to follow the traditional "male" script for a woman's life. George Sand dressed as a man; George Eliot lived openly with a man married to another woman. Indeed, using a pseudonym (as Heilbrun has done herself, as Amanda Cross) or becoming a "fallen woman" has freed many a woman to pursue the life she chose, rather than the narrow role society handed her.

WRITING A WOMAN'S LIFE is a homage to brave women past and present, and an invitation to all women to write their own scripts, whatever they may be.

"Accessible, engaging and compelling...She celebrates those women writers who had the courage to live beyond convention and who seized their own stories: Charlotte Brontë, Colette, Florence Nightingale...."
The New York Times Book Review

"A sprightly, graceful and sometimes acerbic guide to what we might all aspire to become in life, both as we live it ourselves and as future generations will interpret what we have made of it."
The Philadelphia Inquirer

	SBN	PRICE
WRITING A WOMAN'S LIFE	36256-X	$6.95

Amanda Cross Mysteries

DEATH IN A TENURED POSITION	34041-8	$3.50
THE JAMES JOYCE MURDER	34686-6	$3.50
NO WORD FROM WINIFRED	33381-0	$3.95
THE QUESTION OF MAX	35489-3	$3.50
SWEET DEATH, KIND DEATH	35254-8	$3.50

These books are available in your local bookstore, or order by calling toll-free 1-800-733-3000 to use your major credit card. Please mention Interest Code "JOB 40."

Price and numbers subject to change. Valid in U.S. only.